When A Gangsta Falls for a Real One

A Standalone Novel

By

Ms. Grad Marie

D1374206

About the Author

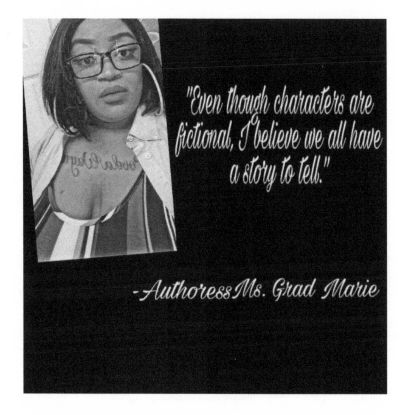

"Even though characters are fictional, I believe we all have a story to tell."

-Authoress Ms. Grad Marie

National Best-selling Authoress Ms. Grad Marie is a Texas native. She writes in a young adult's point of view. Ms. Grad Marie published her first urban fiction novel in the fall of 2017 titled Share my World with A Savage Like You. She now has fourteen titles under her belt with more to come. Ms. Grad Marie began writing at the tender age of only twelve-years-old. Writing helped her escape from her harsh reality.

Ms. Grad Marie's word of advice to new and upcoming authors is: "If it's on your mind...write it off! Pick up the pen and write your way out. And to never, ever, doubt yourself." She enjoys being the mother of two spoiled brats, cooking, decorating, and divatizing.

Keep up with upcoming events & releases via Facebook @MsGradMarie

Contact info: msgradmarie@gmail.com

Acknowledgements

To my Lovies… Thank you, thank you, thank you! You guys have been riding tough witcha girl since I started posting short stories on my page in 2016. I want to thank each and every one of you that support me both near and far! If you would've asked me three years ago if I've ever thought about being a published author, I wouldn't know exactly what my answer would be, but look at me now! I thank all of my Book Lovaz for being patient, caring, honest and there for me and not only with my books! I thank you all for loving Grad just for who she is! AGAIN, thanks for your continued support my loves!

Would you like to be one of Ms. Grad Marie's Lovies? Join my readers group to participate in sneak peeks, discussions, giveaways, monthly contests and more!

Click the link to join!

https://www.facebook.com/groups/169607740478558/

Also, Please like my Author page on Facebook!

https://www.facebook.com/MsGradMarie/

P.S. Here's a link to the character visuals for this novel.

https://bit.ly/2okyu6I

Synopsis

O'Shara and Enzo have been together since they were kids. After years of multiple infidelities, possible children from outside relationships and her first love not being able to hold down a steady job, O'Shara finally realizes that she deserves better. When she meets a rough around the edges gangsta named Rashaan, he shows her the way a true queen should be treated. And it makes her question her relationship with the only man she's ever known and loved.

Charaty, O'Shara's best friend, is torn between her daughter's father and a childhood crush who can only love her in the bedroom to fight off his own hidden demons.

This story of vicious love triangles might end in bloodshed when secret truths are revealed from betrayed souls....

Intro

Light tears stained my puffy cheeks as I swayed my body back and forth to the jams flowing from the speaker that sat on the back of the toilet. My mind kept flashing back to the positive pregnancy test that sat just a few feet away from me on the bathroom counter. I couldn't believe that I was now expecting from the man I'd fallen crazy in love with. I wasn't sure what exact words to say when my boo made it in tonight. But, I was sure I wanted to let him know that I had a piece of him growing in my womb finally after the pain of my body defeating me over and over throughout my life. Who knew, this could be just what we both needed to fix the strain in our relationship. I know that I wasn't perfect and at times he made it seem like someone else had bits of his heart, but I really felt that what we had was real.

I lathered up my loofa with cucumber melon shower gel from Ms. Radia's Spa in a Jar line and gently scrubbed my skin, enjoying the exfoliating fragrance as the calming suds wrapped around my body. Just before I hopped in the shower, my man had hit me up to let me know that he was getting off from work and on his way to me. Being that I had good news to deliver, I spent all afternoon slaving over a hot stove making a few of his favorite dishes.

Knowing that I had about another thirty minutes before he arrived, I decided to lather up my scalp and exfoliate it as well. The pleasant scent opened my nostrils and pores as I massaged my scalp with closed eyes.

"Mmmnnn..." I moaned, enjoying the self-pleasure.

As soon as I stepped back into the flowing water to rinse the suds from my hair, I lost my balance. A strong, muscular arm muffled my screams as it tightened around my air ways pulling me to the slippery bottom of the tub. The soapy water from my head now filled my ears smothering the faint voice I knew I had heard before on many occasions. I kept my eyes closed to prevent the silky substance from burning my vision. My whole life flashed through my thoughts as I wondered why I was chosen as a victim of this foul shit. My assailant lifted me by my neck, ripping away the shower curtain as I was carried like a rag doll to my nearby bedroom.

"I knew you was fucking over me bitch! Oh, you wanna cry now, huh? You weren't crying when you was fucking that nigga though!"

The attacker buried me faced down into my mattress, allowing me to use my bed spread to an advantage to wipe away the irritable chemical in my eyes. After rubbing my face back and forth on the bed, I flipped over and start kicking the monster as he tried to tie my feet up.

"Bitch, I'll fucking kill you, hoe!" The now clear and recognizable speech burst from the chest of the dark silhouette that hovered over my weak body.

"Come on, bitch!" I pumped myself up. "You might can't whoop a nigga ass, but you can challenge him."

I fought back as hard as I could until he thrust his heavy body on top of me, cutting off my circulation by wrapping his hands around my throat. As I drifted off into eternal peace, I caught a glimpse of the man I thought I loved as his hoodie fell back off his head. I was with this nigga through his broke days and when he came up. He was my last and only. I stared deeply into his bucked eyes as I lost my breath, losing all the fight I had inside. I would've never thought that he would be the one to cause my untimely demise.

Chapter One

Charaty

"Bitch, open this motherfucking door!" Armis screamed through my walls. I couldn't believe this nigga was outside my apartment wilding the fuck out yet again this week.

I grabbed my cell phone and kept ignoring his back to back calls as he continued to pound on my door with heavy fists. I hoped like hell that none of my neighbors were outside witnessing this fatal attraction shit. Or even worse, my daughter's father, Samad, who was due to bring her back home in a couple of hours. I quickly opened up my block list and added Armis' number before I scrolled over to my call log to hit up my best friend and ask her for advice in this situation.

"What's up, my snow bunny. I'm just now leaving my job, lemme hit you back when I get downstairs to my car," she answered, calling me the nick name she'd given me when we were kids being that I was bi-racial; mixed with black and white.

"O'Shara Marie Arthur, please!" I begged her, calling her out by her whole government. "Armis crazy ass is at my door again about to kick that motherfucker down!" I cried, slightly afraid of what would happen next being that the disturbance at my front door seemed to cease for a moment.

"Damn, Charaty, again?" Shara huffed, and I'm sure an agitated eye roll came along with it.

We had been best friends for almost fifteen years, since we were only fourteen years old. I was the new white girl in the hood that was hood, so bitches envied me. O'Shara was the only one who befriended me. Shit, it wasn't my fault that I looked like a white girl to most, but my African roots showed the most through my personality. I loved the skin I was in and loved both parts of my heritage. My mother loved hood niggas, so I was just raised in the hood. So, anytime a bitch hated on me saying I was trying to "act black" I beat their motherfucking ass. This is who the fuck I was. I didn't give a fuck if you didn't like it, but you were going to respect it.

"Ok, love. I'ma put you on speaker phone as I go to clock out. You know I have to ride the elevator down to the parking garage, so if I lose service, just call me right back."

I waited patiently for Shara to clock out and get back on the phone to give me some guidance. I wanted to tip-toe from my small one-bedroom to the front door in the living room to check and see if the coast was clear. But I'm sure that Armis' crazy ass was waiting with his ear to the door for my footsteps.

"Fuck! Fuck!" I chastised myself just above a whisper, hating that I continued to deal with this fucked up situation of being torn between the two.

I know my pussy was good, but this cat had to be golden for these two niggas to be tripping the way they did over me. Sometimes I blamed myself. Maybe something was wrong with me and that is why I went through what I did with men and relationships. Shit, watching my own mother get her ass drug down flights of steps and beat up by men who would later on buy her something pretty and say they would never leave her and promise to love her forever, fucked with my mind as a kid. I really thought that shit was normal for real. So, if my baby daddy was catering to me and our daughter, I didn't mind him fucking hoes. And if Armis was dicking me down extra good nightly, I wouldn't let him go either.

"Hello? Hello? You there, best friend?" Hearing O'Shara's voice snapped me out my thoughts, but a little too late. I immediately disconnected the call, ran to my apartment door and snatched it open.

This man had a serious hold on me, and he fucking knew it. Seeing him stand there in his long-sleeve, grey Army shirt that clung to his chiseled, vanilla colored toned body turned my hot pussy ass on. It was hard to stop my eyes from traveling down to his dark colored cargo pants and wishbone shaped legs being that he was bowlegged a bit. Shara told me when we were younger that bowlegged niggas weren't shit but the damn devil.

I stepped to the side and let Armis into my home. He walked in calm, a little too quiet than his usual. I should've known this would be his gentle warning before destruction. He slammed the door behind him, making my front windows shake. Armis glided across my hardwood floors towards me, wrapping his strong man hands around my throat. As my eyes rolled to the back of my head, I got a good view of the clock that hung on my freshly painted living room wall, letting me know that I had a little over two hours to do what I needed to do.

"Didn't I tell yo' dumb ass to stop fucking playing with me?" He spat through gritted teeth.

"I can't. I can't fucking breathe, nigga!" I tried coughing to make Armis loosen his grasp around my throat. Squirming my way out of his arms finally, I was able to crawl to the hallway just a few feet to my bedroom. He quickly snatched me back into my harsh reality, yanking my feet in his direction.

"No, don't run. You've been blowing up my shit all weekend talking about how you missed this dick, so I'm here now, baby. You want it, don't cha?"

I covered my face with both my hands as Armis slowly lifted my dress and removed my purple lace thong from my lower body. I already knew that my little pussy was dripping soaking wet from the altercation we just had. Sometimes I wondered if that's why men treated me so badly. I was used to being treated like shit and dogged out by them then turned on completely by rough sex. Armis placed his soft, pink lips on the pearl of my pretty pussy and pecked her a couple times, making my legs shake.

"I missed her too, baby. Now let's go to the bedroom."

His greased lips met mine and I wrapped my arms around his thick neck, sucking my sweet nectar from them as he carried me to the bed.

***

"Mmmnnnn. Oh, my fucking gawwwddd!"

Lord, why did you have to bless this man with suck good dick? I thought to myself as I gently threw my ass back on Armis' perfectly curved monster he was thrusting in my gushy goodness. I had to say a silent prayer of forgiveness so the man upstairs could forgive me for lusting over this great blessing I was receiving.

When Armis and I made love, it took away all my worries in the world. I no longer cared about my stupid ass baby daddy, the broken relationship my mother and I had or anything else. That nigga had magical dick that took me to places only angels could go. I could feel his stroke speeding up inside me, letting me know that he would be soon coming close to his climax.

I had been fucking with Armis since I was only sixteen years old. It didn't matter to either one of us that he was almost six years older than me. Being a latch key kid while my mother was out bartending and sucking dick to keep the lights on overnight made my house the chill spot for my lil friends in the hood. When the weekends came, my lil potnas would come over to spend the night and this would bring attention to the group of grown ass men who stayed across the street from us.

Armis' uncle's house, the party house as we called it, stay packed with old school gangsters who couldn't wait to get their dick wet in between a young girl's untouched kitty cat just by giving them a nick sack or a couple beers. For the longest, his uncle tried to holla at me, but I just used his ass for the free smoke and buzz he offered. While he was watching me, I was watching his fine ass nephew. Shit, I couldn't help but to fall for that nigga, he was fine as fuck. And to top it all off, when he came to Texas from the boot and I heard that sexy ass Louisiana accent he had, my lil young ass was creaming in my panties before I even knew what a dick was or what to do with it.

One summer, Armis' revealed to me that he was going to the military to make something of himself other than be another hood statistic like his tired as uncle. That was the same Summer I gave him the best going away present ever: My sweet innocence. If I would've known then what I know now, I wouldn't have put this fiya ass cat on that crazy ass nigga. No matter where he went or who he went too, he stayed coming back to me regardless. I had love for Armis' crazy ass, but I was tired of fighting with that nigga just because he knew that I would never leave him the fuck alone.

I snapped out of my thoughts when I could feel the tightening of his shaft as his unborn seeds sprayed from his erect manhood. I moved just in time before he could bury himself deep beneath my birth canal as he did on occasion to trap me into being his for real.

"Charaty! Charaty! Are you in here?" I jumped up when I heard the deep baritone vibrations of Samad's voice.

"Oh, so that nigga got a fucking key?" Armis laughed, slowly taking his time to get dressed, not really giving one fuck if we were caught ass naked.

"Hell no! Yo' dumb ass didn't lock the door earlier, fool," I whispered to him as I ran around my bedroom looking for my dress that was crumpled up on the floor.

"Mama! Mama!" I could hear my two-year-old daughter, Ahmani's, baby voice getting closer.

"You need to hide now!" I mouthed to Armis, pushing him back from the bedroom door as he tried to walk out it.

I stepped out my bedroom door, closing it behind me after pulling my dress over my head, hoping that my bra and lace panties were hidden from Samad.

"Hey, baby girl! Did you miss Mommy? I missed you so much!" I embraced my child tightly, watching the confused look on her father's face, praying that Armis' ignorant ass didn't emerge from my bedroom until he was gone.

"Why the fuck you in here with the damn door opened, bruh? You ain't seen the news lately? So much crazy shit has been going on in the world these days and you got my baby in here with the fucking door opened."

I shook my head and cut my eyes his way. That's one of the reasons Samad and I weren't in a relationship anymore. That nigga was damn near sixteen years older than me and treated me like I was one of his spoiled ass, overgrown children.

"Please don't start your shit today, Samad. I'm not for it, ok. I must've forgot to lock it on my way in. My hands were full, and I was trying to make it to the bathroom," I lied, hoping he would leave the situation alone. Being me, I had to add insult to injury for him trying to check me about my house.

"You complaining about my house like you live here or something," I said with emphasis to piss him off.

"Man, Char, watch your mouth in front of my baby. I pay bills here for our daughter, so I can say whatever I want to say about what goes on in here. Now move out my way. Can I use your shower please and get a nap in? I have to be back on the road to work by midnight, and I'm tired as hell."

I sat the baby down quickly, remembering that Armis was still in my bedroom.

"Why you can't go to one of your lil chicks' house? How you know my man ain't in there?" I joked with him, secretly trying to warn him that my lil piece of dick was on the other side of my bedroom door.

"You ain't that dumb, Char. I know you ain't bringing no niggas up in here while my daughter here. You ain't that crazy." He sucked his teeth and brushed passed me, headed to the bathroom.

I ran into my bedroom to close the other door that was attached to both my bathroom and bedroom. When I walked into my bedroom, Armis was nowhere to be found. I surely hoped that he was hidden deep into my closet, at least until Samad finished his shower. When I heard the shower start, my palms sweated as I patiently waited on him to get undressed and hop in so I could sneak my boo thang out without any bloodshed.

I sat down on my bed and about three minutes had passed. The door swung open to the bathroom and out walked a shirtless Samad. I jumped as I felt Armis' childish ass pull at my feet from up under my bed.

"Damn, I forgot my phone in the car. Where my baby at? Go get her so she won't accidentally walk outside since you don't like to lock doors and shit," Samad spat over his broad shoulders as he walked through the house.

I walked to the living room where Ahmani was playing with her toys and watched her father exit apartment. Knowing that he always parked in the back which was a lil ways down from my apartment, I knew that I had about three minutes to get this nigga out my house before he got back.

As soon as the door slammed behind Samad, I rushed to my bedroom and looked under the bed for Armis' ass. When I bent down to look for him, he was gone.

My adrenaline raced down my body as I searched around looking for him. I heard the toilet flush and darted to the restroom.

"Dude, are you fucking serious right now? You tryna get all of us killed, huh?"

"What? I'on want no damn UTI. You know you 'posed to piss after fucking." He laughed with no remorse. Armis was so fucking kiddish sometimes, that's another reason I only used him for dick. I pulled his arms through the living room before peeking my head out the door to make sure Samad wasn't close by.

"Go! Now! I'll hit your line when he leaves!" I gritted my teeth as I pushed him down the stairs.

"Damn, I couldn't even tell my daughter bye. You wrong as fuck yo'!" He continued to crack up laughing as he jogged down the steps.

I ran back inside and closed the door, then hopped over the end coffee tables to the large window to peep out the blinds. As soon as Armis got to the last step, Samad was making his way back down the sidewalk. I flopped on the couch, grabbing the remote to turn on the TV, trying to look innocent as I caught my breath.

Ahmani heard the theme song to one of her favorite shows and joined me on the couch just before her father came back through the door. As soon as baby girl laid her head down on her favorite pillow, I knew that she would soon be dozing off. I made my way to the kitchen to grab a bottle of water then went into my bedroom to grab my phone. Samad's ass was crazy. Just because that nigga paid for everything, he thought he controlled me as well. I reached across the bed searching for my phone forgetting that I was completely nude underneath my dress. I could feel the wind from the ceiling fan whipping against my backside just before Samad's strong hands wrapped around my naked flesh.

"Baby girl is napping now. Come take a shower with me, with yo' crazy ass," he whispered in my ear. This nigga knew just what his ass was doing. Feeling the vibration of his deep mesmerizing voice on the left side of my neck had my pussy throbbing for more.

No bitch doesn't do this shit. I tried to speak myself out of the horny trance I was in. I wasn't gone fuck this nigga, but I loved the way his strong hands massaged my body when he bathed me. He walked me to the restroom and lifted my dress over my head before pulling me into the steamy water with him.

Chapter Two

O'Shara

"Char? Hello!" I screamed into my purse before pulling my phone out and placing it on my ear. After hearing complete silence, I figured she had just hung up.

I quickly redialed her number and wasn't surprised a bit when I was sent to voicemail. I stopped being worried about Charaty when she called me about Armis' crazy ass. She liked that shit. If being a psycho nigga's punching bag is what made her sleep good every night, I didn't judge. Only time I intervened is when my niece was over there. Then again, Armis knew Charaty's schedule too damn well, so he only did that crazy trip shit when baby girl was gone with Samad for a couple of days.

I figured that Charaty would call me back whenever she finished with her problem, so I made it to my car in the parking garage and decided to go on about my day. As soon as I made it to my lil hoopty, I hit the unlock button on my key chain, and snatched my purse from my shoulder, tossing it in the passenger seat. I sat down in the driver's seat and kicked off my mini heels before reaching to the passenger floorboard to grab my slides.

I was coming up on my two-year anniversary at Sterling Inc and even though I was grateful to have a job, I was tired of the same old bullshit routine daily. Sterling Inc. was another one of the many competitive cable companies that serviced the world. I worked Monday through Friday first shift with weekends off. After a year of being a customer service tech, they finally gave me a funky ass fifty cent raise which put me at 11.50 an hour. Thank God I wasn't blessed to have any children yet because I wouldn't be able to feed them off the crumbs I made.

I buckled myself in and turned on the radio before cranking the ignition and heading to exit the parking garage. I waved goodbye to Stanley, the nerdy, stank breath having security guard on my way down the ramp. As soon as I entered the freeway, my cell started ringing in my purse.

At first, I was against answering the call because I thought it was Charaty with her lies and excuses to why she hung up on me earlier. She knew I wasn't the type to judge her being that I know she had a hard life coming up. But a lot of the shit she went through, she brought upon herself. It wasn't good to cause your own storms then get mad when it rained.

Seeing it was Enzo, my longtime boyfriend, I decided to answer the call. I pressed the Bluetooth speaker on the dash and let the sound of his sexy ass voice flow through my car's audio system.

"What's up, boo? You headed to the house yet?"

"Hey, baby. I'm just now hopping on the freeway with all this damn traffic. What's up with you how's work going?" I tried to keep my cool, but I had been with Enzo's ass all my fucking life, so I knew that nigga like the back of my hand. I could tell from his voice that he was getting ready to give me some excuse to why his bitch ass would be "working late". Any time a man constantly said he was working late, that meant he was working late alright, in another bitches' guts.

"It's going cool. Shit, we're backed up as usual. Three niggas called off today, so I'll be working late again tonight. I'm so sorry, baby. I know you wanted to go see that new movie tonight. I'll make it up to you. I promise."

I rolled my eyes and gripped the steering wheel, gritting my teeth to stop myself from cursing his lying ass smooth the fuck out. "It's cool. We need the money, so it's ok. Besides, the new season to my show comes on tonight, so I'll just watch that until you get home, babe."

"Oh, so you're gonna watch it without me?" He laughed like everything was cool between us.

"Well, I would say I would wait up for you, but I'm kind of tired. Today was extremely busy and corporate was trolling through, so I had to stay on top of my P's and Q's. It's cool, bae. I'll see you when you get home." I brushed my feelings off and ignored him as he apologized again before ending our call.

After being with Enzo's ass almost nine years, I was used to this shit. I dealt with it because the nigga had a legit job, and he treated me good. He was all I ever knew. He was my first, my last and my only. Yeah, it was times he stepped out on me, but what man didn't cheat? If he took care of home, a part of me didn't mind. I couldn't blame Enzo for cheating, if I was a nigga, I probably would too if my girl couldn't hold a damn baby.

An incoming text from my girl Karmyn pulled me out my thoughts.

Karmyn: Wya bitch? What time you leave the slave yard? Come to the bar and have a drink with me.

I rolled my eyes and focused back on the road. Karmyn was an ex co-worker of mine. She worked at the call center with me up until about three months ago. I'm not sure what happened that caused her to leave one day and never return, but a few days after she left, management took her desk computer for investigation and never returned it. I usually don't listen to the gossip around my job because it's almost always a hating bitch that's mad about someone else getting extra hours or a raise. I just did my job, made my lil check and took my ass to the house.

Karmyn: Don't be ignoring me, whore! Look, I'm headed to Reno's. Drinks on me and I got some tea to spill, girl. Here's the address....

I looked at the time on my dash that read 4:30 p.m. and thought about the hour I would be spending in traffic on the way home, plus Enzo working late.

"Fuck it, bitch. Just go," I said aloud to myself and took the next exit. I quickly texted Karmyn back to let her know I would be joining.

In less than ten minutes, I was pulling up to Reno's. I removed my blazer and threw it on the passenger seat. Pulling my visor down, I refreshed my lip gloss, spritzed my body with my favorite body spray and exited my ride. I walked into the smoky establishment, passing up the pool tables and game machines until I got to the bar.

"Hey, babes. What can I get for you today?" The tall, slender, blond-haired, blue-eyed bartender greeted me, placing a small square napkin on the counter in front of me.

"Umm... do you guys have any specials today? I was supposed to be meeting my friend, but I don't see her here yet." I squinted my eyes and looked around for Karmyn again.

"You're K's girl, right?"

I nodded, not really surprised that the bartender knew who I was looking for.

"Yeah, boo, she just stepped off to powder her nose, she'll be back in a jiffy. She told me to fill up your glass with whatever you wanted and put it on the tab she started."

I looked to the right of me at the half empty glass I didn't notice earlier and figured it was Karmyn's.

"Well in that case, I'll have whatever she's having!"

"Peach Zombie with sugar coming right up!"

I sat back and watched the bartender do her thing as Karmyn's long-legged ass came strolling from the ladies' room looking like she had just dipped her pinky nail into a tube of her best friend as she called it and sniffed it up her nose.

"What's up, bitch?" She embraced me, trying hard to maintain her high-pitched voice she'd often put on when she had a fine male audience.

I tried hard not to laugh, but it was so funny to me sometimes. Even though physically born male, Karm was beautiful as fuck. She stood about 5'9 and her year-round, golden tan fully complimented her light, vanilla skin. Her natural mahogany brown inches that she loved to keep straightened flowed just above her slim, tightened waist. Her feminine face was sculpted beautifully as she baked in her mother's womb, destining her to be female. If you didn't know her personally, you would just think that she was a gorgeous woman with a lil bass in her voice.

"Girl, nothing. Just left that hell hole. Ugh, I'm thankful to have a job, but your supervisor be making a bitch wanna up and leave sometimes." I side-eyed Kam, letting her know that her old boss was still with the bullshit.

"Fuck her. Shit, fuck all them hoes down at Sterling Inc. Shit, I'm glad I left that crazy place, girl," she scoffed. Finishing off her drink, she signaled to the bartender to bring us another round.

"Speaking of that. Why did you leave? You know them hoes up there be running their mouths, but I don't listen to the hype. I need to hear it from the source." I nudged her shoulder, hoping she would spill the tea.

"Well, let's just say that it was time for me to go. I let the wrong hoe in on my business and when I couldn't cover her shift when her edgeless ass wanted to go to this kickback in Dallas, she ran her ass down to H.R. and start singing like a bird."

"What did she say? All I know is that you were gone one day when I came in and two days later, management came to your station snatching your desktop wires loose."

"Girl, them hoes didn't have to do all that. I didn't do anything through their system. Well, nothing but get the info I needed," she whispered then burst out laughing. "Shara, let's just say I have this friend who makes credit cards and in order for him to make them, he uses the info I gave him from the customers that would call in to add or update shit to their accounts." She shrugged and started on her next drink like what she just told me wasn't illegal ass fuck and could probably get her ass a five to ten year bid upstate.

I followed behind her, sipping my drink with wide eyes. Part of me wanted to know more as my hands started itching a bit, then the other part of me said, *"Bitch, mind yo mother fucking business."*

"They didn't find any evidence, and I left before they could let me go, so it's done and over with. I just have other ways to pay my bills now outside of Sterling Inc. Bitch, I'm always gon 'eat regardless."

"Hey, boo's, this guy down at the other end of the bar told me to send these over for you." The bartender placed two shots of tequila in front of us. I couldn't see the gentlemen's face clearly, but from his stocky build, wide shoulders and massive blinged out hands, I could tell he was a nigga with money.

"Thank you, love!" Karmyn waved down to the man, clicked my glass then gulped the tequila down.

"Ooooh, I been here already for a couple hours, these drinks running through me. Watch my purse, I'll be right back." Karmyn got up from the bar stool tipsy as hell, knocking over her designer bag in the process. She was so fucked up that she didn't even realize it as she stumbled off to the bathroom.

I shook my head as I got up from my seat to help my girl out, returning the scattered mess to her purse while she took care of her business. As I gathered up the numerous plastic bank cards from the floor, I couldn't help but to notice that Karmyn had a gang of credit cards, and some of them were in other people's names. I hurried up and threw her shit back in her purse when I saw me her long-legged ass bend the corner on the way back to the bar.

"Bitch, I'm lifted. All I want now is some buffalo wings, all flats with ranch and some hard dick." She waved to get the bartender's attention to place her order, but being that Karmyn was a regular, ole girl was already on top of it.

"You want some wings too, girl?" She asked, looking my way with low lashes, indicating she was full of that liquor. Without me even getting a chance to respond, she made sure to shout out she wanted two orders to go.

"When you get a chance, I'm ready for my check! love." Karmyn shouted to the bartender that was down flirting in Mr. sending drinks face.

"Anything else you want, boo?" Karmyn asked, shuffling through the stack of cards in her large hands I had just scraped off the floor.

"Nah, babes. I'm good. Thanks for the drinks and wings. Enzo is working late again, so...." I drifted off, not really wanting to talk about my relationship.

Truth is, I tried to make my nigga look good to my friends and coworkers, but something was telling me that Enzo wasn't always truthful with me. Women's intuition was a motherfucker and she never led me wrong. I just hoped that this time I was over thinking shit.

Chapter Three

Enzo

I tapped on the front door of the customer again to assure no one was home before I decided to leave and head back to the parking warehouse. For the past six years, I had been employed by Southern Freight which was another one of the many package delivery services in the world. It wasn't my dream job, but shit, it paid the bills, kept food in me and my bitch's belly and kept my closet stacked up with the finest sneakers.

Neiysha: Hey, boo. What time you think you're getting off tonight? I would like to see you before you head home for the night.

I re-read the text again before I decided to respond. Neiysha was a lil chick I had met awhile back while on one of my runs; she was on my regular route. She was always ordering shit from Amazon and sometimes, I swore she did that just so she could see my face multiple times a week.

I remember the first day I noticed she was checking for me. She requested a pickup for a package that needed to be sent back, but when I arrived to pick it up, the only thing she had waiting for me was her. She stood in the doorframe almost ass naked with nothing but a g-string on and a sheer teddy. I didn't want to be rude by having her think she was coming off too strong to a nigga or that I didn't appreciate her oh so kind gesture. So I had to spend a couple minutes out of my very busy workday and get to know her a bit. I didn't know that that the flirty meet and greet would eventually turn into a full-blown affair; it just happened.

I fucked with Neiysha the long way though. Her head and pussy game was true fiya, but she was a woman who listened to me. When I was with O'Shara, she would always be cutting me off and shit, thinking I'm lying about everything I said. Shara didn't like to go out anymore, she'd rather stay at home watch movies and chill. Shit, she was pushing thirty-years old, but I had just made twenty-seven with no kids, so I still had my whole life ahead of me.

I wouldn't mind settling down with O'Shara one day, but that being scared to freak me in the bedroom and shy to please her man shit was must end sooner or later. Shara was a bad bitch standing at 5'4, short, cute and thick in all the right places. However, the older she got, the more boring she became. I wanted my woman to have fun with me every now and again, and Neiysha gave me that three times a week and sometimes twice on Sunday.

I texted her back to let her know that I would be sliding through after taking my work truck back to the warehouse for the night. I felt bad lying to O'Shara about working overtime again, but seeing that she didn't respond back to the text I hit her up with after we ended our call, I figured she was in one of her bitchy ass moods again. Might as well go to my other bitch house for a little tender loving care. Shit I wasn't getting the attention I needed at home no way.

***

I pulled my truck into the warehouse and killed the engine. After gathering my work bag and the rest of my undeliverable packages, I headed to the office to clock out. I thought about calling O'Shara to see where her head was at to decide if I wanted to head home, but my mind drifted back to Neiysha and the way she made me feel.

O'Shara and I had been together since I was eighteen and she was twenty. Even though I was a youngin' still wet behind my ears, I had a thing for the older ladies. We both grew up in church, and since our families were close, they always rooted for us to make it. I had been with Shara all my damn life and never really had a chance to experience the single life. I didn't want to leave her alone for good because she indeed was a good woman. Sometimes I felt like I was stuck with her, especially after the multiple miscarriages. We weren't married and had no kids or serious ties, we were just together so long because that's what our families wanted; at least that's how it seemed at times.

I dapped up my co-workers and headed to my whip, contemplating with myself whether to go left to O'Shara's and my apartment, or to go right and hit the freeway to a night full of good head, no nagging, no bitchin' and some good sticky Kush. I sat at the stop sign on the corner stuck in a daze until one of my coworkers behind me laid on their horn, pulling me out my thoughts. I followed the feelings of my dick head and bust a right, headed to the freeway that led me to a night of pleasure.

About twenty minutes had passed before I pulled up to Neiysha's apartments. I liked the fact that her shit was sewed up with security, so my ride wouldn't be fucked with. And the complex was so large that I didn't have fears of running into anyone I knew. I found a parking spot along the visitor fence, jigged out my ride and grabbed my duffle bag from the backseat before checking my surroundings and speed walking down the sidewalk that led to Neiysha's crib.

Me: I'm here, boo. Open the door.

I texted her to let me in, ready for the surprise she had in store for me. Most of the time when Neiysha said she needed to talk to me, she talked alright, with her lips to my hard dick. Within seconds, she pulled open the front door and shocked me. She was fully clothed and not scantily clad rocking some see-through shit that had me ready to poke her thick ass as usual. She pulled my arm and quickly closed the door behind me.

I walked to the sofa and plopped down, not too comfortable with the vibe I was feeling. Usually when a nigga came through to drop dick off, she had some soft music in the background with candles and shit, and a plate waiting in the oven for me. I didn't know what was up, but I hope it wasn't any fuck shit popping off because me and my bitch Nina stayed ready.

"Hey, baby. Sorry I didn't get a chance to cook tonight, I should've asked what you wanted and picked you up something. Would you like a drink?" Neiysha scurried to the kitchen to make us both a double of cognac without waiting on my response.

I walked over to the dinner room table and took a seat, trying to read her to figure out whatever she had going on. She emerged from the kitchen smiling with two glasses of ice and sat them both down before she took a seat and filled them both to the rim.

"I-I don't know how to say this, but I have a proposition for you. And I don't want to jeopardize your job or anything but..."

"What's up, boo? Spill it." I took a swig from the glass and gave her a pierced look. She was sitting there like she knew some shit I didn't know about. Shit, I hadn't been this nervous since my old broad I was fucking on the side a few years back revealed she was pregnant. Made that hoe get an abortion though. I would never hurt O'Shara in that way. Neiysha took a deep breath and continued.

"Ok. My cousin Thugga, remember I was telling you about him?" I nodded, urging her to continue.

"Well, he's back in town for a lil minute. He dropped by earlier and asked if I knew anyone that would be interested in making some extra money."

"Making extra money how?" I raised a questionable eyebrow in her direction.

She finished her drink, refilled both our glasses then connected eyes with me. "Thugga is the connect, remember I told you that before."

"OK, what's up?" I was starting to get agitated with her ass.

"All he needs is for someone to deliver "Packages" to the loading dock on the Eastside every two weeks when the guys that work offshore come and leave. Two weeks on, two weeks off."

"And what does that have to do with me, Neiysha?" I lifted the liquor to my lips and slowly sipped as she went on. I cut my eyes at her over the glass.

"I felt that it would be easier for you to do it because of your job. And he's willing to pay you five hundred dollars a week." She nodded and pursed her full, sexy ass lips. I didn't know if my monster in my joggers started expanding because of the gesture that graced her beautiful face, or the amount of money she just dropped to my knowledge.

"So, you're telling me that all I have to do is drop his shit off every two weeks and I get paid weekly? That doesn't add up, ma."

"Yes, that's his interest and service charges. He knows that it's risky, but all you have to do is make the drop to the dock every other week to the foreman on board and you will get your cash in hand for every drop. You don't even have to deal directly with Thugga, I'll take care of all communication." She smiled to soften up the fact she tried to hit a nigga with the okey doke.

"Man, I don't know about this shit. Like, what if shit goes left man? I ain't tryna be locked up, bae."

"Enzy, you know that I wouldn't let anything happen to you, baby." She rose up from her seat and straddled my lap. Placing my hands on her fat ass booty, she pulled me deeper into her devilish trap.

"Baby, just think about it okay. I told Thugga I would let him know by the end of the week. The first shipment comes in two weeks. He even left your first deposit here to help you easily make your decision." She pulled five crispy blue bills from her bra and fanned them in my face.

I attacked her neck with my tongue and stood, wrapping her legs around my waist and walked her to her bedroom. Throwing her on the large bed, watching her crawl to the edge and pull at my joggers turned me on. As bad as I wanted to push my hard inches down her delicious throat, I couldn't stop thinking about what I had at home.

"I can't tonight, baby. I'm sorry. I promised my Mama that I would stop by when I got off to help her with something." I lied hoping that Neiysha didn't ask me with exactly what because at the moment, I couldn't think of shit.

"It's ok, boo. I understand. I'll just have to pull my Purple Peter out and get to work!" She laughed as she reached in her nightstand drawer for her vibrator.

I placed a sweet, enduring kiss on her forehead before walking down the long hallway to retrieve my bag and dip. I turned the lock on the door handle and closed it before making my exit and jogging down the steps. On the way down, I saw an extremely intoxicated couple walking in the apartment below Neiysha's. I wasn't one to judge but ole dude liked chicks with dicks, or the female was just tall as fuck with manly hands. I shook my head and walked back down the sidewalk the way I came.

On the thirty-minute drive home, I debated with myself whether to take Thugga's offer or not. Shit, wasn't nothing wrong with having a lil extra bread.

Chapter Four

Karmyn

I could barely get my apartment unlocked and opened before my trade's hands wandered all over my body.

"Hold on, bae, let me go slip into something more comfortable ok." I had to pry his strong hands from my Miami made derriere before I could run off to my bedroom.

Trade niggas, better known as masculine, down low brothers, were the best to fuck with any given day. Most of the time, "secret" gay men paid you better treatment than openly gay men because they paid like they weighed to keep their trapped in the closet ass secrets safe.

After scurrying to my bedroom, freshening up my kitty and putting on a cute nighty, I returned to the living room to entertain my guest. I wrapped my arms tightly around my trade's neck and pulled him closer to me.

"Aww, baby. I can see you wasted no time getting ready for this pussy huh. You wanna go to the bedroom, or you want your woman right here on the table?" I teased him, walking over to the dining room table and tooting my ass in the air.

He came to me and swaddled me in his arms from behind. Taking no time to remove my lace panties, my trade pulled them to my ankles and dropped to his knees. I rolled my eyes to the ceiling trying to hide the uncomfortableness I felt as I did many times before when he tried to give me head.

My little friend that I was born with was the only thing stopping me from feeling like a complete woman. I had a gorgeous face, flawless body and plump ass, but the pool stick and balls that hung between my legs reminded me daily that I wasn't living as my true self. I told my trade time and time again that I wanted to find the best doctor in any hospital to burn the manhood the world identified me as to dust, but he was against it. I gritted my teeth and cringed every single time my trade wanted to play with his little friend down there.

"What's going on, Karm? Am I being too rough, babe? I'm sorry, I just missed you so much while I was away at work, but it seems like the feeling isn't mutual." He stood, locking eyes with me while continuing to rub on my limp shaft.

"Of course, I missed you, honey. It's just... well, you know." I walked a few steps from him, trying not to upset my money bag.

"Look, baby cakes, I've told you time and time again that I love you. All of you, just how you came. Many people are blessed with something special and having you is like having the best of both worlds. And I-I wouldn't change it for anything in the world, Karmyn."

He came to me and began placing kisses on my hot spot on my neck, not helping much with the way I felt.

"I just want to be all woman. You know, 100%. I told you that knowing that piece of my past is still there brings nothing but hurt to my heart. I'll never understand why you are so infatuated with it." I crossed my arms, hoping not to start an argument, but I needed for him to hear me loud and clear. I didn't ignore his feelings ever and I would be glad when the day came that he respected mine.

"Babe, I told you that you are my first and only different woman. That makes you super special to me. Now I don't know if the reason my dick stays hard is because I know yours is there, but I love every part of you. If you remove that little piece of you knowing that I love it so much, I don't know how I'll feel. When I met you, I took you exactly as you were. I fell in love with you for all of you."

I knew that he loved me for me and that's one of the main reasons I fell for him. Well, that and his hefty bank account. No matter how much I hated my penis and the thought of another man getting pleasure from going down on me, I loved the way my trade felt about me and reminded me every chance he got.

"See, that's what I'm talking about, baby cakes. Now you're in the mood." He smiled looking at my semi-erect penis and dropped back down to his knees to finish what he started. He didn't know the reason for my soldier saluting was because of the words he spoke to me from his loving heart, not because I was into this shit.

Just breathe, bitch, and think happy thoughts so you can continue to get your weekly allowance to save up for that pretty pussy one day.

I closed my eyes and thought about how sexy my body would be after I was surgically transformed into the real woman I was born to be. I continued to fake moan until my trade's warm throat made me climb to a climax.

Chapter Five

Samad

"Aye, boss man, what's up, you called for me?" I put my clipboard down beside me on the desk I was sitting on and directed my attention to my foreman.

"Yeah, Roberts, I did. Have a seat for me please." I walked around to my desk, closely watching the body movements of my second shift supervisor.

Roberts was one of my best workers. He worked overtime every time when asked and the team he oversaw were some bad ass underwater welders. I met Roberts back when I had first got out the penal system. I did a 6-year bid upstate back when I used to be the man of my neighborhood. When I stepped into that familiar court room expecting my usual slap on the wrist, I was shocked finding out the news from my overdressed, well-paid lawyer that Judge Smith was no longer playing with my ass. It hurt like hell when I had to sign for that decade and leave my two teenage kids behind. Thank God for mercy and parole. When I came home from jail, I straightened my life up, copped a welding trade and made a better life for myself and my children.

A short while after working as a welder, I met Charaty's crazy ass at a Stop N'Go gas station. Her beautiful ass was sitting there looking all distraught because she had a flat tire and didn't have the first clue on how to change it. So, me being the handy guy I am, I chose to be there for a damsel in distress. She offered to pay me a dub for helping her clueless ass out, but I refused and told her she could repay me by joining me for lunch at a local bar. We hit it off quick as fuck and soon, she was my lil young dip, just a few years older than my kids. I could tell that she had a troublesome childhood, but I never judged her on that and never would.

I loved Charaty and wanted to have a lengthy future with her, but she needed to grow up a bit. I know Mami was young, but with me, she had nothing to worry about but school. I would always keep her and Ahmani well taken care of. When she moved out and chose to get her own apartment, it hurt a nigga like shit. But in the long run, it might just draw her closer to me after seeing what it feels like to miss something good. I didn't want to pressure Charaty, but I did love her crazy ass. Something was telling me that she was fucking with somebody else. I didn't think she would do any foul shit in front of our baby girl, but bitches could never be trusted these days no matter how well you knew them.

I worked offshore three weeks on and one week off, so it's no telling who was busting them guys open. Shit, we weren't fucking, and I couldn't remember the last time we did. So, I would keep doing me until she decided to do us. I snapped out my thoughts of my baby mama and chopped it up with my foreman.

"How much longer you think that job gon' last tonight?"

He looked down at his watch then back up at me. "Shit, them boys said about another six hours or so. They prolly down there bullshitin,' riding the clock and shit. I'ma go check on them in about another hour."

"So, what's been up with you and wifey? Shit she coming out when we dock in Louisiana next week or what?" I poked at his brain, noticing how his demeanor changed.

"Man, I don't know shit. She been acting funny with a nigga lately. She probably got a young piece of meat dropping it off in them drawls while I'm over here sweating my ass off. I don't even care though shit. It's cheaper to keep her. If the nigga ain't laying up where I pay the bills at, I'm straight."

One of his crew members called on the radio needing assistance.

"I ain't want nothing much, bruh. Go ahead and handle that."

He dapped me up before making his exit. I pulled my desk drawer out and grabbed the small velvet ring box I had been holding for the past almost six months. I know that I was a man with a corrupted past, but I turned my life around. When Charaty and I first met, things weren't perfect and I was still out in the streets doing my thing with multiple women while she sat at home and took care of the house. I just wished that she would see my mass improvement and stop judging me on what was.

I admit that I liked the way hoes looked at a nigga with bread and wanted me for my money, but I've seriously outgrown that mentality and lifestyle. My oldest kids were grown now, and I wanted Ahmani to grow up in a positive and loving two-parent home. I gave her and Charaty everything they'd ever dreamt of. No matter what I did for them, she would always hold over my head the long nights I was out entertaining bitches while she sat at home, especially while pregnant.

I didn't bother to look at the ring I bought that was almost half a month's pay. I tossed that shit back in the drawer and slammed it shut. I made my way down to my room and found my cell to hit up my homegirl Khandi who worked in the kitchen.

***

I closed my eyes tightly to stop them from rolling into the back of my head.

"Sssss, girl, fuck!" I shouted out like a lil biatch as Khandi's head bobbed up and down on my hard dick. This girl's head could put Pinky the porn star outta business.

She lifted my member up to my navel and hummed on my scrotum as she alternated popping each one of my balls in and out of her mouth. The slurping sounds followed by moans she made let me know that she was enjoying pleasing me just as much as I was enjoying getting pleased. Sweat beads formed on my hairline with guilt as I looked down at my ringing phone that showed "Baby Girl" across the screen. *Fuck, girl, not now baby,* I thought to myself while trying to hold back the spew of creamy kids that were about to erupt from the mushroom tip of my manhood.

Khandi stuck her tongue out and rubbed the tip of my piece up and down her moist lips. She put my dick on her shoulder and moved back and forth to massage the bottom of it with her beautiful, caramel skin as she flicked her tongue across the top. My phone stopped vibrating and it seemed as soon as it did, I exploded. My dick went limp in Khandi's mouth. I palmed her pretty brown round and rubbed it in my hands as she licked up the mess she created in between my legs.

Even though I sometimes felt guilty for fucking with Khandi, I gave my baby mama the world and she acted like giving her man some head every now and then or letting me fuck her in spontaneous places was a problem. I even tried to get Charaty to fly out to our base since we were off on weekends, but she refused. She always acted like school was more important to her than me needing to see her and our child. I loved her with all my heart and that's why I was planning to ask for her hand in marriage. It ain't like I was stepping out on my girl. Me and Charaty broke up officially six months ago when her and baby girl left to get their own apartment. Maybe me being torn between what I wanted and what I had in the past was wrong, but so was me giving Charaty part of my check and not being able to have her like I wanted to. She knew she had a nigga, and no matter what, I would never stop loving her and providing for them.

"You gone call her back? I can step out and take a shower," Khandi offered. And that was another reason I fucked with her. She knew her place and stayed in that shit as long as I took care of her, making sure her check showed overtime pay for hours she spent making me feel good.

"Yeah, I'll be in there in a second," I told her and watched her ass while she walked away.

I had to shake my head. Khandi would've been perfect for me if she could get it through her thick as skull that this was a no-strings attached thing. Yeah, I know I was just talking shit about giving Charaty a piece of my check and her working and trying to get her education, but I knew that those were all things that would make her a great wife one day. And even though she constantly reminded me of my wrong doings in our relationship, I could get her to finally see that I was working on that.

I may be wrong for the way I was handling shit right now, but I also knew that you don't give up what you have at home for a work fling, and that's some real shit. Yeah, sex and quality time were important to me, but Khandi didn't offer shit else. And she was free all the time for the sex and quality time 'cause she had no ambition. If I could have 'em both, that would be a win for ya boy, but that shit wasn't gone fly with Charaty. It barely flew with Khandi. I still hadn't told Khandi I planned on marrying Charaty 'cause as cool as she played about being on the side, I knew she had feelings for me, and that shit wouldn't go over well. I'd have to tell her eventually, though. Just… not right now.

The phone rang again, bringing me out of my thoughts. I looked at the screen and it was Charaty calling back. Wiping my hand down my face, I hit the answer button on the video call. Imagine the shock I got when I saw her in the tub, sipping a margarita, wearing nothing but a smile.

"Well, hello to you, too," I said with a smirk. She was being extra nice today because it'd been awhile since she did anything like this for me. Maybe she could be everything a nigga needed.

"Hey there, baby daddy. Judging by that smile, you like what you see?" She blushed, taking another sip from her glass.

"You know I do. What do I owe the pleasure of this kinda treatment?" I asked, and she bit her bottom lip trying not to focus too much on her big, soapy titties.

"Well I called earlier because Mani was asking about you, but now she's sleeping in her bed. So, I knew if you had called back, you would want to see she was sleep and I wasn't bullshitting your crazy ass."

"Whatever, Char. If you just missed a nigga a little bit, that's all you had to say," I joked with her.

"Wellll...." She started making me blush and totally forget that I had my side pussy showering just a few feet away from me.

"If you missed me, you would come see me on my off days, Char. You don't miss me that much 'cause you can't make time for me. Yeah, school is important, but you can study anywhere. You don't think I miss you too? I hate not seeing my daughter for weeks at a time."

She looked like she wanted to cry and that made me feel bad. I didn't mean for it to come out like that, but guilt was getting the best of me. Khandi felt good as long as I was down her throat or all up in her guts. But when I got mine, I wanted my family. So, her not being with me sometimes made me angry. But that didn't justify me taking it out on her.

"Wow. Well, tell me how you really feel," she said, trying to hide her hurt behind her attitude. It wasn't working though because her eyes were glossy, and I could tell the tears were coming. I had to find a reason to get off the phone because I hated to see her cry. And worse than that, I hated for her crying to be because of me.

"It's not that, boo. Look, I just really be missing y'all. That's it. Yeah, I'm working for us but... Look, I'm sorry, that didn't come out right. I—"

"Save it, Samad. I'm gonna let you go. Next time I miss your ass, I won't waste my time letting you know. And to top it off, here I am trying to show you my feelings that you've played with too many times before and you couldn't stop being an asshole long enough to enjoy it. I hope you have a good night. I'll have Ahmani call you in the morning when she wakes up," Charaty said before hanging up the phone.

It had to have been the liquor that gave her the courage to speak to me like that. It had been a minute since she went ham on a nigga. Nah, it can't just be the that. It's the liquor, loneliness, and the fact that she knew she had a fucking hold on me. My older kids' Mama never made me feel about a woman the way I felt about Charaty.

I was about to call her back, start beggin' and try to open up my heart to her when I looked up and saw Khandi standing in the doorway to the bathroom with her arms folded over her large, perky breasts, naked as the day she was born. I thought she was upset that I'd missed a round of fucking in the shower, but then her mouth told me the real reason behind the scowl on her face.

"Oh, so you out here caking on the phone with bae, huh?"

"Ain't no bae, I'm single as fuck and you know that."

Damn, how much of my conversation did her nosy ass hear? I thought, knowing that both women in my life were about to be on some bullshit tonight.

I didn't respond, I just looked down at my phone, waiting for it to ring like it always did when Charaty got mad at me, and I didn't call her right back. I almost needed the phone to ring, so that I didn't have to face Khandi. *Come on, Char, call back.* I tried to woo her, but to no avail. After about a minute of silence and Khandi staring a hole in my head, I finally let my eyes meet hers with that beautiful, innocent face of hers twisted up into a scowl. *Oh well, here we go*, I thought to myself with a sigh.

"Yeah, that's my daughter's mother, so of course I give a fuck about her, but we ain't together. And me and you ain't either. When were together, we're together. And when we're not, we're not." I admitted, waiting for the yelling and screaming.

When she broke into tears instead, I didn't know what to do. I didn't expect that reaction. I mean, I knew that she was gonna feel a way, but crying when she knew I had a life back home. That was one of the major problems with this offshore life. Some people didn't understand that work was just that, work. I could never have anything serious with someone I worked with. What did she really think was gonna happen between us?

I sat on the edge of the bed and watched her chest heave, her nose and eyes leak with water, and her body start to tremble. I couldn't make out what she was saying, she was wailing so bad. I knew it was coming from a place of hurt. From a woman who really thought that if she fucked me just right, I was gonna leave my life back home for her. Watching her suffering at my hands and knowing that Charaty was feeling the same way, I knew I had some making up to do with both. I would start with Khandi.

You know how the saying goes, *If you can't be with the one you love, love the one you're with.*

Chapter Six

O'Shara

Two Weeks later...

I stared at the vase of rainbow roses that sat on my desk from Enzo. Reading over the card he sent with them had me blushing hard. It had been a long while since he sent me "just because" gifts, so I was enjoying every bit of it. At first, I was against him working all these extra hours, but seeing how it brought in more money to our household, I dealt with it. The extra money he was bringing in, he used to treat me to lavish gifts and saving for our dream home.

I desperately wanted to try conceiving again, so I had been looking into seeing a fertility specialist who could help me along my journey. After seeing that the first round of in vitro fertilization would cost over $17,000 and it was not covered with my insurance, I began to tally up just how many hours of overtime I could work in order to at least get enough for a down payment. Either my eyes were playing tricks on me, or my handy dandy calculator was playing games with my emotions. I didn't want to work my ass off for five years just to get the one thing I've always dreamt of.

"Hello, Sterling Inc., how may I assist you today?" I was interrupted by a beep in my ear from my headset letting me know of a customer. I pushed my thoughts to the side and listened to their request as I waited on my computer to pull up their account information.

Working at a call center, you had to have tough skin. Throughout the time at my job, I had been called every name in the book from disgruntled customers who were upset when they couldn't get their way. Most of the time they blamed the employees for the reason they couldn't pay their cable bills. It wasn't our damn fault that they thought cable was a necessity. I guess sitting on your ass watching scripted brawls on television from celebrities who give one fuck about their fans didn't was more important than anything to them.

"What did you say your name was now again, baby?" The elderly lady spoke just above a whisper on the other end of the line.

"O'Shara. My name is O'Shara, Mrs. Williams."

"Oh it's Ms., baby. I'm not married anyone. I'ma widow. The good Lord took Wilfred home 'bout fifteen years ago. So, it's just me and our son. The grandkids come by sometime, but I haven't been Mrs. Williams for a long time now."

I rolled my eyes and gritted my teeth as she went on. This was something usual that happened with older customers. I knew and understood at a very young age that sometimes things happened beyond our control, so I would just let them vent. Hell, as annoying as it was, it helped my time on the clock pass by. I looked down at my cell seeing that I had a little over three hours left in my shift. Maybe if this old bat kept running her mouth about her deceased spouse, that could knock out at least one hour.

As soon as I sat my phone down, it vibrated from an incoming test message.

Best Friend: What time you get off, bitch? You been acting funny, but me and Mani still love yo' ass.

I smacked my lips before responding. I wanted to read Charaty's ass because she knew why I was distant with her. It wasn't easy to care for Armis knowing that he treated my friend like crap. Part of me blamed Charaty though because she liked that crazy shit. I told her repeatedly to let that crazy ass nigga go, but she was stubborn as fuck. Yeah, Samad fucked up in the past, but he was trying to do right by her. That nigga wanted to give her and my lil niece the world and I believed him because I could see it in his eyes. Shit, if Enzo told me I could stop working and just be barefoot and pregnant, I would quickly turn in my headset and badge without a question and pop out as many babies as he wanted.

Me: Girl, whatever. Tell Nanny baby I'ma try to come see her when I get off later. And I love y'all too, y'all know that.

Charaty: Ok, boo, just hit me up. You know I got some tea for you, girl.

I sat my phone down and exhaled. I really didn't want to hear shit about Armis' ass I missed Ahmani and wanted to see her, but now I wasn't so sure because I didn't want to hear about her possible father. I loved my girl Charaty, but she really needed to get her shit together.

I tuned back into Ms. Williams who continued to ramble in my ear about her lengthy love and marriage. My computer dinged from an insta-chat from my team leader, Johnny.

Johnny: Is everything going ok on this call?

Me: Yes, everything is fine. Just another elder calling in for aid then went off on a tangent lol.

Johnny: Ok, not trying to be rude to her, but this lengthy call will mess up your stats for bonus payouts. Try to help her out with the reason she called and wrap it up.

Me: No problem.

I smiled back toward Johnny's desk as I cut off the caller. "Yes, Ms. Williams, that all is so wonderful to hear. Now is there anything else I can assist you with today regarding your service?"

"Oh, yes, dear." she laughed. "I'm so sorry, sometimes an old woman like me just rambles on. Next time, just cut me off, baby. Yes, I was calling to add that package I saw on the TV screen last night. The one with True Crime with the shows that tell you how to kill people. Now I don't want to kill anyone, but I like watching it. Can I have a senior citizen discount?"

"Sure, Ms. Williams, I can add that package for you. All I would need is your credit card information for verification and after your seven-day trial, it will be added to your account for an additional $ 2.99 monthly."

As the customer gave me her information, I thought back to my last meeting with Karmyn. We texted each other from time to time since we'd met up, but it wasn't anything serious. Thinking about the cost of motherhood and seeing the crumbs I made every couple weeks intrigued me to learn more about Karm's little credit card business. I didn't want to steal anyone's identity or anything, but I was curious to know just how much more money I could make if I silently partnered with Karmyn. After finishing the call with Ms. Williams, I logged out and took a ten-minute break.

Me: Hey, boo, what's up? Call me when you can please. I have some questions about what we were chatting about that day at happy hour.

Me: I'm interested in making some more-

My text was interrupted when my cell rang from Karmyn's call.

"What's up, bitch?" Her deep voice screamed through the phone, making me pull my cell from my ear. I walked out the building and made my way to the parking lot where my car was.

"Hey, boo. What you been up to?"

"Girl, nothing, just trying to balance these niggas." She laughed. I'm not sure where she was but her background was loud as fuck.

"Karmyn, girl, you so crazy."

"One more for the road Suzie, then I can close my tab out."

"Oh, so you at the spot getting fucked up." My hands perspired as I waited on her to respond to my earlier text.

"Yeah, girl, I'm leaving Reno's. And I got your message so when can we meet up and discuss business?"

Remembering I had promised Charaty I would visit today after my shift, I figured I could meet up with Karmyn on my next off day. After deciding when we would meet up, I returned to work to finish off my shift. I returned to my station and pulled up the last five accounts of customers who called in to make payments. Looking over my shoulder, watching my team leader as he visited other supervisors, I quickly took down the information I needed on a note pad in my phone. I closed my screen and took the next call just in time before Johnny came back to my station to check on me.

"Shara, it's kind of slow today. If you want to leave an hour early, that's fine."

I looked at the clock seeing that I had a little over an hour left. I hated missing money, but it was almost my Friday, so I was ready to get the hell outta the building and into some more comfortable clothes. I closed out of the system and logged out my account ,saying my goodbyes as I walked to the front of the building. I texted Charaty as I hit the freeway, seeing what she had in her pots so I could get my grub on as she ran her mouth about the two niggas she was torn in-between.

***

Almost twenty minutes later, I pulled up to Charaty's apartments. She lived on the other side of town from Enzo and me. We didn't live in the hood but not far from it. We weren't making money like Samad who financed Charaty's luxurious lifestyle. She didn't have to work for a living, but she was enrolled in school to be a paralegal. I was proud of my bestie for wanting to make something of herself, especially for her daughter.

I parked in the designated area for visitors, grabbed my purse and phone and made my way across the parking lot to head to my friends' crib. I could feel the stares from a fine ass, milk chocolate, buff brother who was standing shirtless in front of an oversized truck he was wiping down. I forced an uncomfortable smile and slightly waved at him when he noticed me gawking at his fineness as I walked by. He gave me a head nod, pretending not to watch me as I made my way around the bushes to my friend's house. Before I could even knock on the door, Charaty pulled it open and embraced me.

"Damn, bitch, you act like you haven't seen me in forever. It's only been a couple weeks."

"Oh, girl, shut up. I missed yo' crazy ass. You know I ain't got no friends, but you bitch. Let's have a seat, so I can lace you up on what's been going on."

"Aht, aht, bitch, what's in these pots? I'm hungry. And why you didn't make any drinks?" I comfortably kicked off my shoes and made my way to the kitchen to raid her fridge.

"I was going to make some, but Mani just laid down. She's been sleep for about an hour now. I made some nachos though, feel free to help yourself."

"Oh, bitch, you know you don't have to tell me twice. Let me go wash my hands."

I made my way to the bathroom, and Charaty pulled my shirt collar and pointed to the kitchen. She knew I didn't wash my hands in anyone's kitchen if I wasn't cooking. I brushed her off and tip toed to her room to freshen up. After I washed my hands and dried them, I tip toed to Charaty's bed and saw that Ahmani's eyes were open, but she was still laying down.

"Mani," I called just above a whisper to let her hear my voice. I didn't care about nothing her Mama was talking about. This was my baby and I missed her.

As soon as she saw my face, she shot up in the bed and extended her arms for me to pick her up. I swooped her in my arms and carried her to the kitchen.

"Really, Shara?" Char grunted and rolled her eyes. "I should've known yo' ass was gonna wake her."

"Nanny miss her Mani. You wanna eat, Mani?"

I sat down at the table while Charaty showed her hospitality and fixed me a plate. She buckled baby girl into her highchair and made us some daiquiris as I fed the baby.

"Bitch, ya boy really been on some trip shit lately."

"Who is my boy, Samad?" I sarcastically responded, knowing she was referring to her crazy ass side-piece.

"Girl, hell no. You know who I'm talking about. Quit being funny. I'm tired of him coming over here tripping. When we first moved here, I didn't tell him where I moved to, but guess who I saw one day while I was checking the mailbox after school one day."

"Ouch! Mani, you gon' bite yo' Nanny." Ahmani almost took my finger off with her baby teeth when Charaty revealed that Armis' crazy ass was now her neighbor.

"Wait. What the fuck do you mean?"

"You know who lives out here. And not just out here. Like same building same row! He's like three doors down from me but downstairs." I continued feeding the baby with one hand and chugged my drink with the other while shaking my head.

Char knows I didn't judge, but she was setting herself up for a death sentence. Armis was crazy, but I'd never seen Samad go crazy and that's what I was more afraid of.

"I told yo' ass to cut him off already. You're playing a dangerous game."

"But I'm single, girl. I'm not in a relationship or committed to either one of them niggas-"

I cut her off mid-sentence. "That's what you're telling yourself and me, but if y'o lil hot pussy ass keep fucking both then no matter what, you belong to them. Armis is crazy as fuck, so why do you keep him around anyway?" I asked, cutting my eyes in her direction. Watching her put her head down, I knew more excuses would soon be flowing out her mouth protecting his psycho ass. Now I know my relationship wasn't perfect and Char saw firsthand some of the bitches I had to deal with Enzo fucking with on the side, but I wasn't playing with fire.

"I haven't cut him off because.... because he might be Ahmani's father."

"Bitch, what?!" I almost choked on my food. I looked at the innocent baby who was just smiling away, not knowing that she was a pawn in this dangerous game her mother was playing.

I hadn't seen Armis in a while. I usually got ghost when he came around because of the vibe he gave me. But sitting there looking at the freckles that graced Ahmani's nose, they were identical to his. And when she looked up at me and smiled, my mouth dropped.

"Let me find out that's why you named her Ahmani?" I shot her a confused look, kind of disgusted with what she had just told me.

She nodded her head and rested her elbows on the table.

"Armis knows he's a possibility, but Samad doesn't. I told Samad that I stopped fucking with Armis about a year before I got pregnant with Mani. But as the days pass, she looks increasingly like that nigga to me. And if he is her father, I can't deny him a relationship with her. That's why I let him come by when he wants to see her."

"To see her or to see you?" I exhaled deeply, rising from the table to throw my trash away. I returned with wipes to clean off the baby, turning my back to Charaty to avoid her face and feelings. She was so wrong, and she knew it. I'd hate to see things turn for the worse, and the child ended up fucked off in the long run. That's all I cared about.

"I know you don't care for Armis much, but he looks out for us. I don't like asking Samad for shit all the time because he tries to hold that shit over my fucking head. So, when he's acting like a bitch nigga, I call Armis to get shit taken care of."

"Ok, Char. I understand. I just want what's best for Mani. You know that's all I care about. Thanks for the food and drink. I got to get home because I have an early 12-hour shift tomorrow," I lied, wanting to get the fuck from around her now.

Charaty could be so selfish at times and that's something I hated about her. I wonder what kind of golden dick Armis had that made her feed into his bullshit constantly. I kissed Ahmani and hugged her before giving her, her sippy cup.

"I'll text you when I make it home babes." I called over my shoulder as I exited the apartment.

I had an uneasy feeling as I walked back to my car in the parking lot. I didn't speak on it because I didn't want to make Char feel even worse, but I noticed the bruises on her arms and neck. I knew they didn't come from Samad because that nigga had been away at work the past couple of weeks. When we video chatted the other day, I thought that maybe it was some bad lighting where she was sitting but seeing that shit in the flesh let me know that my feelings and suspicions were correct. I was starting to hate that bitch ass nigga. And a part of me resented Charaty too for allowing herself to put up with that bullshit.

I made it to my ride and hit the unlock button.

"So, you can't say goodbye?"

Feeling the liquor flow through my system and feeling some type of way about my best friend, I ignored the male voice and continued to open my car door when he stopped me.

"Oh, so that's how it is, ma? Shit, I bought you and your homegirl some drinks at Reno's that day and you couldn't even come down and speak then either. I'll let you go then, be safe, ma."

"Huh?" I stopped myself and looked back at the man. It was the same fine motherfucker from earlier that was half-naked, oiled up and staring me down.

I didn't get a good look at his face that day at the bar, but I would never forget his well-manicured, strong hands.

"Oh, that was you? I'm so sorry, I just-- I just got some shocking news from my best friend, so my mind is kind of allover the place right now."

"That's cool, Mami. I'm Thug- well, Rashaan. What's your name?"

"My name is Shara. O'Shara." I blushed at him.

"So, what's up. I would ask if you got a man, but that's none of my concern. As fine and as thick as you are, I would be surprised if you didn't have one. All I need to know is can I have your number?" He licked his full lips and I tried hard not to stare at his sexy ass beard that had my pussy throbbing under my skirt.

"How about you give me yours?" It had been years since I had been noticed by a man and hit on. He made a bitch feel like I just got my groove back.

"If you ain't gon' use it then don't take it, ma." He pulled my cell from my hands, completely ignoring the screen saver of me and Enzo boo'd up and put his number in my phone. He made sure to call his phone from mine to get my number as well.

"A'ight, ma. Im let you go since you're in a hurry. Be safe, beautiful."

We said our goodbyes, and I watched him watch me through my rearview mirror as I exited the complex. I shook my head at myself. I couldn't believe that I had just judged Charaty for juggling two guys and I could easily be in the same situation.

Chapter Seven

Thugga

Beautiful Shara: I made it home, Rashaan. I'm about to get ready for bed. Have a goodnight.

Me: Thanks for letting me know, love. You have a good night as well, beautiful.

Thinking about O'Shara's beautiful ass had my lil nigga rock hard down below in my sweats. When I first saw her pretty ass at the bar with her homegirl a few weeks back ,I wanted her. But shid, the way she jetted out that day made me feel like she had a curfew or something. I was stunned when I saw her earlier by my crib. I thought that I would never see her again. Being back in town, I needed a something warm and soft to cuddle up with from time to time. I didn't wanna be all up in shorty business, but it did grace my mind just who she was out here visiting. Whoever it was must've upset her because she walked in straight and came out abruptly with a definite change of demeanor.

I walked to my closet and threw a hoodie on top of my wife beater. After sliding some ankle socks on, I walked to my spare bedroom to count the bread I had to drop off to my kinfolk. I didn't know much about the nigga she set me up with to deliver my work, but I trusted Neiysha. She knew firsthand that I wasn't the nigga to play with. I would have no problem lighting her ass up and whoever the nigga was that was dropping my shit off.

So far, homie had already made two runs and my boy Roberts didn't complain of any shortages, so everything was good with me. I had no problem putting bread in anyone's pocket if they worked for it. I didn't even know lil homie's name and didn't care to know if he carried out what I paid him to do.

I opened my safe, loaded my strap and tucked it in my waist. I counted out the stack of bread for Neiysha and put it in my bag. Being sure to lock up my safe and apartment before dipping, I headed down the steps to my whip.

I was thirty-five years young, no kids, no bitch, no wife, and after working offshore for a few years, I decided to go back to what I knew; the street life. I was an only child, raised by a single mother. Most of my life, I traveled back and forth with family between Texas and Louisiana. The offshore gig was cool for the first couple years, and the money was straight, but that routine shit got boring to a nigga after a while. I felt like I could move more weight off the ship, so the next time we were scheduled to return to work, I just didn't show up.

I wouldn't mind having a steady relationship one day, but that wouldn't be successful working all those hours in the sea. I saw firsthand how plenty of them niggas were out there paying for pussy and shit. They didn't give a fuck about the wife and family they had back home. I just wasn't down with that shit, plus, I wasn't paying a bitch to fuck me.

About thirty minutes later, I pulled into Neiysha's complex. I shot her a text as soon as I parked to let her know I had arrived.

Fam: Ok, cousin, let me know when you are coming down the sidewalk so I can unlock the door for you. I just hopped out the shower.

Me: Bet. I'm coming down now.

I jigged out my truck and made my way down the dark sidewalk. I liked how quiet it was around her spot, but that also let me know that I needed to stay alert because no matter what, someone, somewhere was always watching other people bit'ness.

When I got to the end of my cousins' staircase, a tall, familiar looking woman was coming out Neiysha's door. I waited like the gentleman I was, letting her come down the stairs and so I could get a good look at her face.

"How are you doing, love?" I spoke, ignoring her response as I took the stairs up two at a time. I knew I had saw that chick before somewhere but couldn't quite out my finger on it.

I tapped on my fam's door twice before twisting the brass knob and letting myself in.

"Cousin, is that you?" Neiysha called from her bedroom. I sat down at her dining room table waiting for her to come down the hallway.

"Aye, who you got up in here?" I scratched the back of my head, reading her face for her response.

"Ain't nobody up in here, Rashaan. My girl Karmyn was just leaving after bringing me some business info."

"Yeah, whatever." I sucked my teeth viewing her scattered office of credit card fraud that was all over the table next to her laptop.

I brought Neiysha $1500 weekly for her to split with her lil homie for helping me out at the docs. $750 a week was more than enough to keep her wanna be bougie ass afloat. Plus, she got an SSI check from her deceased ex. She was young, single and had no kids. I don't know why she insisted on playing with old folks' money and identities, but hey that wasn't my problem. She finally came and joined me at the table.

"So, how's everything been going?" She asked with wide eyes, watching me pull the crispy blue presidents from my bag.

"Yeah, everything straight, kinfolk. Bit'ness is good, no complaints yet."

"Cool." She smiled, firmly gripping the Benjamin's out my hand.

"I don't want to overwork ya potna, but I might have something else opening up for him soon. Kind of in the same area, but I don't know yet. I'll let you know though."

"Straight up. So, what's up? What you got planned for tonight?"

"Just business as usual. Might go pick me up a meatloaf plate from Ms. Grad's kitchen then back to the house and watch the game."

"Now how you gon' find you somebody and you always in the house? I'm sure one of these lil hot pussy that's out here would love to be your woman."

"See, that's just it. I don't want these hot pussy thots. When it's time for me to settle down, it'll happen. Right now, I ain't worried about nothing but my bread. And the only bitch I need on me at all times is Nina."

"Well, I'm going out tonight if you want to join. It's this new lil spot that just opened downtown. It's chill and laid back, not a club. They do like spoken word and shit, or are you too much of a gangsta for that?" She tapped my arm and burst out laughing.

"Nah, it's cool. I can dig it, but I'm chilling tonight. Maybe some other time." I stood and looked over the table again, making sure her fraud ass hadn't stolen my identity. That was my first cousin and I loved her, but I didn't trust a soul that walked God's green planet.

"You be safe, cuz, I'll see you after the next drop."

I made sure she locked the door behind me and jogged down the steps. I tried to push back my thoughts about O'Shara. After I thought about it, I wouldn't mind taking her on a date or something. I didn't know if she was into poetry, but I would pretend to be just for a night to pick her beautiful brain.

When I got back to my ride, I started the engine then pulled out my cell and opened my message thread. I wanted to text her just to start a conversation, but I knew that she was probably in bed being that it was almost midnight.

Fuck it Shaan, I boosted myself up to hit her up anyway.

Me: I know you headed to bed to get all your beauty rest, but when can I see you again? We can go out to eat or have a drink, just let me know when.

I threw my truck in drive and hit the freeway. My cell lit up from an incoming text message.

Beautiful Shara: Ummm... I'm not sure if that can happen.

Before I could respond to her text, my phone rang. Seeing it was O'Shara, I answered on the first ring, eager to hear her explain more in detail what she meant.

"What's up, beautiful?" I answered, waiting on her response.

"Hey, I--"

"Hello?" I called into the phone again before looking at the screen and seeing that the call was lost.

I quickly redialed her line and didn't even trip when I was sent to voicemail. I shook my head then focused back on the road and my plate I had already called in. I knew Mami was too damn fine not to be some nigga's gal.

Chapter Eight

Neiysha

"Aayyeee! Shake that ass bitch!" I tapped Karmyn on her plump booty as she twerked it in the air. She was really entertaining the crowd of horny, nothing ass niggas that surrounded us.

I continued to be her hype woman because it kept the free drinks flowing from the packed club full of niggas who probably didn't know my friend had the same shit in-between her legs as they did. Shit, it was 2019, and these niggas these days were open to that shit anyway.

After my cousin left my crib, Karmyn and I had gone by the poetry spot, but the turnout was weak. And with the new fit I was rocking, I had to be seen by somebody since my nigga was playing house with his bitch. So, we decided to head to this lil spot downtown that was hosting three parties. The music was banging, the crowd was thick, the niggas was fine as fuck, and everybody was vibing in their zone.

When the current song ended, Karmyn finished clapping her cheeks and grabbed my arms, pulling me off the dance floor.

"Girl, I got to piss bitch, let's go to the bathroom."

We made our way to the lady's room, ignoring the stares from the edgeless wacky dressed hoes on our way there. After getting inside the packed lady's room and handling my business, I decided to text my lil boo thang to see what he had going on.

Me: Hey what's up, boo? I know you're probably tired from work. Just wanted to let you know that I missed you tonight and I got your stuff. If you can, come by and see me after work tomorrow.

I knew when I first met Enzo that he was in a relationship, but that's what made me want him even more. Knowing that I had piqued a taken nigga's interest was the shit to me. A lot of hoes these days claimed that their dudes were untouchable and would never leave home. The truth was a sideline bitch had a nigga better than the main bitch did sometimes. Yeah, those girlfriends, baby Mama's, and fiancées got their man's checks, but us side hoes are the ones that had them niggas' mind and feelings.

One of the main reasons a dude stepped out on his bitch was because she was lacking in something. With Enzo, I couldn't quite find out what it was. But I was doing something right that made that nigga lie to his bitch about working late constantly. I kept quiet when he would be on the phone with her or pretended as if I was sleep while he sold her broken promises and empty dreams to make her feel good. I didn't give a fuck about how that bitch felt. She practically threw her nigga in my lap by not doing her job as his woman.

Enzo was fine as fuck standing 6'3, weighing 240lbs of all muscle. His perfectly toned body made his work uniform cling to it and that's what drew him into my curiosity. Well, that plus seeing the way he tucked that medium baby snake in his work shorts. They say everything happens for a reason, so it was for me to meet him the day I received the wrong package. Little did we both know, he was the right one. We got to rappin' and that's how it happened. Now all these months later, he was the only man who occupied my vacant kitty cat.

I snapped out my thoughts and refreshed my lip gloss as Karmyn emerged her skyscraper-built ass from the restroom stall. After she washed up and checked herself in the mirror, we were headed back to the dance floor.

"Oooh, bitch, I'm tired and hungry. Let's go by the diner and grab some grub or something."

"Cool, boo, I'm with it." I followed her out the club to her flossed out ride in the parking lot.

Karmyn told me before that she was some older married nigga's sugar baby. So, that big nigga paid like the fuck he weighed making sure she stayed draped in designer, had the best foreign hair from all over the country and all her bills stayed paid. That didn't stop her from helping me out with my credit card business though. Shit, you could never have too much money. And we were trying to live our best life before either of us were welcomed to Parenthood.

"So, what's up with your homegirl you were telling me about? She ready to start making some money or what?" I asked Karmyn as we walked to her ride. I slid my cell back into my clutch after noticing Enzo read but hadn't responded to my text message.

"Yeah, girl, she's down. She just wants to provide us with victims, and we can pay her a lil cash for each person she gets or whatever if that's cool."

"Excuse me, Ma. Aye, wait up!" A male voice called behind us. I was used to niggas hitting on my homegirl when we went out, and I didn't blame them because Karm was gorgeous as fuck.

I grabbed her keys and hit the locks, then pulled open the passenger door and slid in. I cranked up the a/c while she had a quick convo and exchanged numbers with the dude. My cell vibrated, alerting me of a new text message from my lil dip. As soon as I clicked to open it, my whole mood changed.

Lil Dip: Ok I'ma be by to get that when I can. But we gotta talk about some shit soon though. Idk man, I just don't want to get caught up between you and my girl.

I started to fly off at the mouth and read the shit outta his ass but decided against it. I knew one thing though, if Enzo expected to keep making bread on the side through my cousin Thugga, the only way he would is if he kept fucking me. Something told me not to trust that nigga completely anyway, and that's why I took off my lil $250 in interest weekly without him or Thugga knowing it.

"A'ight, boo. A'ight, I'ma hit you up for real. Let me get my girl home to her kids. Her mama already calling tripping," Karmyn told her usual lie to bugging ass niggas who wouldn't leave her alone after the club.

"Bihhh, now why you lying to that man? He's kind of a cutie though." I looked over at the skinny, but sexy motherfucker that was hounding my friend as he finally walked off.

Karmyn threw her ride in drive and sped out the parking lot.

"Girl, I had to get away from that nigga, shit. I just gave him my number and he already asking can we kick it like damn, smh. I'm telling you they be hooked on this boy pussy. I know he felt my dick when I hugged him twice. Shi,t all that twerking earlier made me sweat off my duct tape down there. That's why I can't wait to get this shit chopped the fuck off."

"Girl, yo' ass is crazy. Let's go eat though, I want some waffles."

"Ok, boo, I got you," she said, looking over her shoulder as we entered the freeway.

"He light skin, but he must be African or something with a name like that." She laughed.

"Name like what, hoe? What's his name?" I tried to keep the convo with my homegirl going to keep myself out my feelings.

"Armis. Girl, whatever that shit is. I thought he said Otis at first."

We both cracked up laughing.

"He bowlegged as fuck though, so I know that dick good."

Chapter Nine

O'Shara

Three weeks later...

I scrolled through me and Rashaan's message thread. Seeing his past Good Morning beautiful messages and how he checked on me throughout the day just because had me blushing. I wasn't quite sure how to reveal to him that I was in a relationship. That's why the last day we communicated, I blocked his number, so I wouldn't be tempted to call him and lead him on.

I'm sure that by now he had figured the shit out or had met someone else. I couldn't even trip on it though because things were going good between Enzo and me. For the past month, he had been working his ass off and making sure he spent time with me. I hadn't told him about the little business arrangement I had with Karmyn, nor did I plan to tell him.

Our anniversary was coming up soon, and I had been trying to figure out a way to put it in Enzo's ear that I wanted us to try for a baby again. Since I was off for the day, I spent my time cleaning the house and doing laundry. I had a couple ribeye's marinating in the fridge so I could serve up some surf 'n turf with a lil side booty and some good head for my man when he got off later.

As I sat on the sofa watching my favorite True Crime shows, I thought about how things were getting better between Enzo and me. Our relationship was far from perfect. And since we've been together all these years, he's had a few moments of infidelity that made me question myself about whether I was enough woman for him. After seeing how both our parents were still holding on over thirty years later, I knew that our love and bond was strong enough to do the same.

I never thought about spending my life with anyone else but the man I loved. Honestly, I'm not too sure why I gave Rashaan my cell phone number that day I left Charaty's. I guess now I appreciated that all my luscious curves were still attracted to and appreciated by the opposite sex. I had a coworker who was a stud that hit on me all the time, but I paid Nikko no attention because she flirted with everything walking. Sometimes when you felt neglected by your spouse, you looked for that attention in the wrong places from someone else. I understood that as a man, Enzo thought he was supposed to always be the sole provider. Especially growing up with his mother as a housewife and his father slaved down at the office daily. I tried to explain to him many times that we were in this together, and even though most of our relationship I was the bread winner, I would never throw that shit in his face.

I brushed my thoughts off, hopped of the couch and headed to the kitchen to start dinner. As soon as I slid the marinated steaks into the oven, Charaty was video calling me. I wanted to ignore her call being that she had already texted me three times pretending like she cared about what I had going on when in truth, she just wanted to ramble on about her psycho ass side nigga. I tried to be that friend that didn't judge, but the shit was getting tiring.

A real friend wouldn't sit back and continue to bring toxic shit your way after you've already told them how it made you feel. I'm not saying my best friend was toxic, but that abusive relationship she was in drained me for her. I didn't give a fuck how good a nigga dick made me feel if he was putting his hands on me. That shit wasn't cool at all, especially since my Mani was around. I shook my head, pressed the button on my phone to answer her call and turned to the sink to wash my hands.

"Ayyyeee, Bestie, what's up? Wait. Where's your face girl? All I see is all that ass in the air." Charaty cracked up laughing, and I joined her.

I started twerking in my soft pink moo dress to entertain her a bit.

"Girl, yo' ass is crazy. Where my baby?"

"She over there with her people. Shit, I needed a break. These summer classes kicking my ass. I don't know what the fuck I was thinking taking this shit. Everything is just so rushed. I hate it. But anyway, what's up in them pots, bitch!"

She sat up and got closer to the screen, looking around my kitchen.

"Well, you know I'm a fantastic chef in my off time, so I'm whippin' up a lil steak and potatoes for me and bae, ya know." I gloated as I began peeling the freshly boiled veggies, proudly looking over the delicious creation I had put together.

"A'ight, a lil steak and B.J. for my boy Enzy. What time he gets off? And why you didn't come visit me today since you were off?" She rolled her eyes and pursed her lips at me.

I hit her ass back with the same sarcastic eye roll before I answered her.

"Shit, he should be on his way home shortly. And girl, I was so tired and had a lot of housework to do, so I've just been napping off and on, doing chores and stuff."

"Ok, boo. It's cool, I understand. S.J 'posed to be dropping Ahmani off in the morning. I might just call up my lil boo thing and see if he wants to come over and Amazon Prime and chill."

I blocked out her comment about Armis and went straight to more important things which should be her top priority, her daughter.

"That's good, friend. Shit, you been busting your ass in school, so you deserve a break. What my Mani doing over there with her big bro and sis-in-law? That's good they have a close relationship despite the age difference."

I took a playful jab at Charaty, secretly making fun of Samad's old ass.

"They were having a birthday party for S. J's son, so they decided to keep her for the weekend. So, you know, if you're not busy tomorrow on your last off day," she emphasized. "You should spend some time, you know, with your bestie of... I don't know .... Ummm, the last fifteen years."

Even though at that moment Charaty was being sarcastic, I knew she had been hurt by my distance lately. I swallowed the lump in my throat and decided that I was going to spend the next day with her. I will also let her know exactly how I felt about the dirty game she was playing. If she loved me, she would know that I was coming from a sincere place.

"I will let you know, boo. I promise."

"Mmn hmmn," she sarcastically responded before going on about school stuff as I finished preparing my meal.

I loved that Charaty was in school for law because she was helping me learn a lot in this crazy world and fucked up ass judicial system. I learned something new daily through our talks when she vented to me about school. It was vital information for your everyday life, so I took heed.

"Damn, it smells good as fuck in here, baby. What you are cooking up, girl?"

Enzo startled me as he came through the door of our apartment thirty minutes earlier than expected. He wrapped his strong arms around me from behind and began to place soft kisses on the side of my neck.

"Eww PDA!" Charaty gagged on the phone as she watched us.

"What's up, Char? Where that lil mean ass baby at?" Enzo joked with her as he stole a piece of broccoli from the pot on the stove.

"She with the people. I'ma tell her uncle Enzo asked about her. Well, y'all enjoy dinner and hit me up tomorrow, Shara. I'm about to shower and go to bed alone since I have no company."

"Girl, you crazy, Char. Alright, boo, I'll hit you up in the morning. Love you, babes."

"Love you too, thick'ems." We said our goodbyes and ended the call.

"So, how was work, babe?" I turned from the stove and asked my man, trying to hide just how turned on he had me being in uniform. As he stood at the kitchen bar looking through the mail he had just picked up from the mailbox, my eyes traveled all over his perfectly toned body.

I don't know what the fuck it was about men who worked delivery jobs, but all them niggas looked good as fuck in them tight ass shorts that stopped just above their knees and showed all the junk they carried in their crotch.

He shook his head. "All this damn junk mail." He walked over to the trashcan and tossed the many pizza coupons and unopened envelopes of car warranty offers inside of it.

"It was cool, boo. Just another day and another dollar. Shit, I'm glad I didn't take those extra hours tonight though, a nigga tired as fuck. And I'm hungry too."

"Well, baby, after I finish peeling these potatoes, we can grub. Everything else is done and ready. Do you want to shower first before we eat?"

Enzo walked behind me again, making sure I felt his thick meat hardening against my backside.

"I wanna eat first, baby. You… come on."

He pulled the peeler from my hands and sat it down on the stove before leading me to the bathroom just past our bedroom. He reached in and started a steamy shower, then took no time pulling my moo dress over my head. Watching my erect nipples with unblinking eyes, he ripped off his work uniform and crumpled it on the floor, making my pussy leak in satisfaction.

I sucked in my bottom lip, letting out heavy breaths as Enzo dropped to a squat, pulling my hot pink, lace panties down with him along the way. He licked his first two fingers before sliding them into my love box and wrapping them around my quivering pearl tongue that begged for his lips. He spread open my thick, coochie lips gently then dove headfirst into my dripping kitty cat. I grabbed ahold to the towel rack that was behind me tightly, almost ripping it fro the wall. He pinned my body up against it, forcing my legs open as he palmed my cheeks to support the balance of the both of us. I gripped his freshly waved up taper as my eyes rolled to the back of my head, making me moan in satisfaction.

"Ahhhhhhh, Enzy, mmmmmmnnnn." I could feel myself creeping to my climax, but I didn't want to disrespect the wonderful dome I was receiving by cumming too quick. I gritted my teeth and let the intimate tears drip from the corners of my eyes, no longer able to hold back the eruption of my sweet cream that was peaking from my soul.

Without further ado, I exhaled deeply, letting my built-up tension loose, making myself squirt all over my man's beard. Hearing the way he continued to grunt and smack on my flesh let me know he was thankful that I was satisfied with my pleasure. He finally released the death grip his mouth had on my flesh and sat me down gently. I opened one eye and looked around the steamy bathroom, refusing to let myself come back to earth from the cloud I was floating on.

"You good, boo?" He asked, taking a towel to his face to clean up the remnants of my feminine juices that glazed it.

I nodded my head and laughed as I walked to him to suck the rest my succulent nectar from his tongue. Remembering that I had food on the stove is the only thing that snapped me out of the heavenly trance I was in.

"Go head and get in the shower, babe. We're gonna finish this when I get back." I winked over my shoulder, exiting the bathroom.

"Hold up. Where you going, baby?" He called after me, pulling me back to his sweaty chest.

"I gotta turn the oven off so I won't burn dinner."

"Ok, boo. Hurry the fuck up. He's waiting on you." He slapped me on my bare ass with his hard, curved dick.

"I will, babe." I watched him slide the curtain back and disappear into the shower as I scurried down the hallway, heading to the kitchen to turn the oven off.

As soon as I turned to head back to our bedroom, Enzo's cell he left on the counter started vibrating back to back. I walked to the bar to retrieve it, thinking it could be important, then stopped when I saw what was laying underneath his phone. I picked up the small stack of papers that were his check stubs. My eyes bucked viewing his "overtime" hours he claimed he had been working and seeing how they weren't documented on this paperwork. They damn sure weren't showing in his weekly payout either.

Chapter Ten

Charaty

I called Armis' cell again when he sent me to his voicemail for the fourth time that night. I wasn't sure what the fuck that nigga had going on, but I was amped up, ready to slide down my steps and stomp my ass on over to his apartment down the sidewalk from me.

Me: Well fuck you too and whichever one of your hoes you're laid up with tonight, bitch ass nigga!

I tossed my cell on my bed and drug my feet to my kitchen, searching my freezer for the bottle of tequila I had picked up earlier. I had taken a break from studying and since Ahmani was still gone for the weekend, a bitch was lonely. I understood that O'Shara had a man and a relationship, but lately she had been distant from our friendship. No matter what I went through with the niggas I was torn in between, I still always made time for my best friend. Shit, I had to, she was around before both them niggas came in the picture.

I looked under the kitchen cabinet in search for the blender when a knock on my door startled me. I started to go back to my bedroom to retrieve my cell phone to see if my visitor could've been Armis' ass after I cursed him out through several text messages. I sat the liquor down and rushed to the door when I heard my best friend's tear-filled voice on the other side of it. I snatched the door open and pulled O'Shara into my arms out of the stormy weather.

I snatched up her duffle bag that sat at her feet, closed the door behind me with my hip and walked her over to the sofa to sit her down. She didn't even have to tell me. I could already sense by her upsetting demeanor that Enzo's ass did something fucked up. This wasn't the first time that nigga did some foul shit, and the way Shara acted as if she was head over heels for him, it probably wouldn't be the last. Sometimes she was so quick to judge me for having two niggas, but shit, I had to protect my heart. If one nigga wasn't acting right, then chances are the other one was.

"I was just about to make some drinks. Sit here, let me go blend them up right quick." I tapped my bestie on the knee before standing to head back to the kitchen.

"Uh, friend, I don't want anything frozen right now. I need mines on the rocks so I can take it straight to the head."

"Ok, boo."

I went in and grabbed the chilled bottle and two glasses. After filling a small bowl with ice and grabbing a chaser, I made my way back to my friend with my arms filled, hoping I could ease her pain. Shara snatched the bottle from me, popped the top and filled her glass. After swallowing the tequila in one gulp, she exhaled and sat all the way back on the couch shaking her head. I followed behind her, filling my glass but only halfway and taking a shot.

"Bitch, can you believe that this nigga back to his same bullshit?" She started, making my eyes widen.

Over the years the two had been together, it wasn't uncommon to find out that Enzo was stepping out yet again. That's another reason I did me. Couldn't no nigga have me tied down and expect me to accept that he was a cheating dog too. Fuck no! I'll take a couple of niggas for $200 Alex.

"What happened, friend?" I asked, full of concern. Never would I fix my lips to say I told you so to my friend, but the more Enzo fucked over her, the more I wouldn't respect his trifling ass.

"Too much. He promised me that he would stop with the lies and shit, but I don't trust him. Some shit is just not adding the fuck up, hoe, like for real." She huffed and crossed her arms, cutting her eyes my way.

"Like, Math was never my strongest subject in school, but I know that if you are working all these "extra hours" as you say, it would show up on that check."

I pursed my lips to stop what I wanted to truly say and filled my glass up to the rim the second time.

"What, Char? Say what you gotta say because it's clear on your face," she laughed uncomfortably.

I shook my head and shrugged my shoulders. "I don't know what to say honestly. Maybe it's not that bad," I lied, trying to comfort my friend. We both knew that the number one way for a man to try to hide his infidelities is to say he's working late.

"You say that he's been spoiling you lately and bringing in more money, so could he be getting paid under the table or something?"

"Nah, I don't think that's it. I think that nigga has resorted back to his old ways. If I find out Enzo is back in the streets working for his tired ass cousin dealing drugs, I'ma slap the fuck outta both. Char, I can't go through that shit again. Those long nights sitting at the house wondering if that nigga safe out there in those streets and having to call his daddy to bond him out time and time again. I'm over that shit. I refuse to go through it again. I really felt that he was back on the straight and narrow."

I wrapped my arm around Shara's shoulders and let her vent without judgement.

"Everything is going to work out just fine, boo. Just watch and have faith." I encouraged her, unwrapping our embrace when I heard my cell ringing from my bedroom.

I speed walked from the living room to my bedroom, hopping across to my bed. Pulling the pillows off and the covers, I searched for my cell like a hidden treasure, hoping that Armis was the one hitting me up. To my surprise, it was just Samad's worrisome ass. He knew that baby girl was gone for the weekend, so I'm not too sure why he was ringing my line this time of night. As I walked back to the front of the house, I saw that Shara was standing at the door with her bag on her arm and her phone on her ear. I shook my head, not wanting to ask any questions or judge her. I knew by how she rushed to the door that Enzo's lying ass was on the other end of that phone threatening to harm himself as he usually did when he did some fucked up shit.

"I gotta go. I'll call you later," O'Shara said just above a whisper, placing her phone on her shoulder to cover the speaker.

I shook my head and rolled my eyes as I walk into the kitchen. I was being stood up by my best friend, my side nigga and my daughter. I snatched the bottle of tequila from the counter and took it to the head. Walking to the front door, I slid my feet in the pair of slides Armis had left and snatched my front door open.

I had one thing in mind, and that was heading I've to his apartment to see what bitch he was boo'd up with that caused him to ignore my calls and play with my fucking patience. I had time today!

Chapter Eleven

O'Shara

"Baby, where the fuck is you at? What are you tripping on me?" Enzo whined in my ear as I exited Charaty's crib.

I didn't mean to walk out on her like that, but at this moment, I was in a fuck everybody mood.

"Dude, fuck you right about now. You ain't shit but a fucking liar. You promised me that you would do better and get back on the right track."

"What the fuck is you talking about, bae? Bring your ass back to this house, man, a nigga gotta get up early for work man. I don't have time for this fuck shit. You are tripping over nothing. A nigga don't be lying, I be at work."

I blew air out of my nose and gritted my teeth, not wanting to listen to any more of his lies.

"Fuck you, Enzo. I saw your pay stubs. You been doing something to get extra ends but working extra hours ain't it, nigga. I was born on a night, but not last night. Fuck you! Goodbye!"

I pulled my phone from my face and stormed down the sidewalk.

"Wait! Rashaan!" I hurried to the parking area when I saw him scurrying to his truck. He turned on his heels and gave me a confused look.

"Who me?" He pointed his thumb to his chest and sarcastically looked to his sides. "Hello, O'Shara. How are you doing? I'm surprised you even remembered my damn name." He laughed, showing his perfectly pearl-colored straight teeth before looking me up and down then walking away.

I felt embarrassed and bowed my head just in time, realizing I hadn't hung up on Enzo just yet. I smashed the red phone icon and threw my cell in my bag. I slowly walked to Rashaan's truck behind him as he jumped in the driver seat of his pickup. I couldn't be mad if the nigga no longer wanted to fuck with me. I shouldn't have dissed him. He turned to me after sitting down and dangled his leg out the truck while scrolling down his phone.

"Look. I'm sorry, Rashaa,n ok." I started, not sure where to go with the conversation. Even though I chose to stop communicating with him a few weeks back, I did start to miss our convos. "I- I've just been going through some things." I tucked my hair behind my ear and fondled with my phone, feeling that I was bothering him.

"It's cool. We all get busy with life. Shit, I'm getting ready to head out of town now to handle some shit."

"Ok. It was good seeing you again. Be safe, love." I waved to him awkwardly before turning and stepping away, feeling like I just got slapped in the face.

Why couldn't I have met this nigga nine years ago, shit? Here I was being faithful to a nigga who couldn't even be honest with me, and there were so many men all over this beautiful world that were ready and willing to treat me like the queen my mother birthed me as.

"I will, you be safe too. Oh, and Happy Birthday, beautiful!"

Chills filled my bare arms and goosebumps went down my spine. I almost fainted when I became short-winded as I ran back to Rashaan's truck. Just as I lifted my fist to knock on the window, I could hear him throw his whip in park before he rolled the window down.

"What's up, boo? Everything straight?" His big brown eyes cascaded over my surprised face, wondering what he did wrong.

I sucked in my full lips, trying hard to control my emotions that wanted to overflow now.

"You-you remembered! You remembered my fucking birthday and my own best friend and--" I stopped my words, closing my eyes to attempt to hide the thick tears that flowed from them and traveled down to my trembling lips.

"Whoa! Wait, baby girl. Uh uh, we don't do that." He jumped from his truck and pulled me into his strong embrace.

"What's up, boo? Did I say something wrong?"

I shook my head and clinched his chest, feeling the beat of his heart flutter uncontrollably. I shook my head and took in the moment as he rocked me in his arms, not caring who the fuck was around us could see.

In less than twenty-four hours, I would be turning the big thirty, and not one of the people in my life who I gave my all to uttered a word about my special day. All Charaty wanted to talk about was her piece of dick. To be honest, it hurt like hell that Enzo didn't mention it earlier but was ready to get a nut out from me. I was done being underappreciated; it was time for me to know my fucking worth.

"No, Rashaan. You've never done anything wrong." I stepped back and looked into his chest brown eyes that stared back at me, showing that he had so many hidden treasures behind them. "I just can't believe that you're the only one that actually remembered my birthday, that's all. You're the only..." my words drifted off and I buried my face into my hands and started balling again.

"Boo, please. I'm sorry. I didn't mean to make you cry. Stop it now. I know that your family and friends have something special planned for you. Maybe it's a surprise or something." I appreciated him trying hard to make me feel better, but the more he went on, the more my heart stung.

"No, not at all. But thank you, for-for at least remembering. You go ahead and get on that road and take care of your business. I'll go treat myself to dinner and drinks or something and attempt to celebrate."

I pulled out of his arms and wanted to walk away, but he pulled me back to him.

"Nothing is worse than having to spend your birthday alone. How about you ride with me?"

"Ride with you? But to where? And you know I must be at work bright and early Monday morning, so I don't know." I crossed my arms and shook my head watching his facial expression change.

"See, you're asking too many questions, girl. I just gotta run back home quick. I see you already got a lil night cap bag and anything else you need, we can pick it up. Look, I'll pull your ride into my parking spot, so the office won't be tripping 'bout yo' shit being parked in the visitor's area too long."

He intertwined our hands, took my bag and walked me to the passenger side of his truck. After opening the door for me and making sure I was settled, he jogged around to the driver's side and hopped in to pull closer to where I was parked.

"Gimme your keys, boo." He pulled them from my hand without waiting on my response.

As I watched Rashaan take over, I felt like a huge weight was lifted off my shoulders. Even if it was temporarily, or just for the weekend, I was going to enjoy the one person who gave a fuck about me in this world. Reaching that age was an important milestone that my family and one and only devoted friend should've been ready and willing to celebrate with me. I had completely forgotten that through our many long conversations on my breaks at work and constant text messages that I had told Rashaan my birthday.

After he got my car situated, he hopped back in his truck and we were on our way down the freeway. I didn't know where he was taking me, nor did I give one fuck. All I knew is that the way I felt at that moment, I never wanted anyone to take it away from me.

"Click it or ticket, boo." Rashaan laughed as he looked over his shoulder to switch lanes.

I pulled my seatbelt his way to show him that I was riding safely. I felt so cared about, so secure, and so wanted. I had never been kidnapped before, but for this weekend, *my* weekend, I was going to enjoy being the top priority on someone's list for once. I sat back in the seat, slipped my shoes off, and tucked my feet up on the door beside me.

"That's right, boo. Get comfortable, we'll be there in a couple of hours or so. You smoke?" He asked, ready to pass me the rolled up dro and lighter.

I laughed. "Well, I haven't smoked since high school, but shit, I need to hit that after the week I've had."

"Ladies first." He winked at me, smiling as he passed me the funny, yet soothing smelling tobacco.

"Thanks."

I lit the tip and inhaled deeply as the smoke filled my chest, then blew it out and started coughing.

"Yeah, that's some real shit from my Cali connect. That might be too much for ya, young blood," he teased me. "You good? Need me to stop and get you some water or something?"

All I could do is nod my head because I was still coughing as my eyes watered. I passed the weed back to Rashaan, figuring I wasn't about that thug life.

"Cool, I gotta gas up anyway." He pulled into a nearby gas station and killed the engine. After hitting the square a couple times himself, he jumped out the truck and shook in the door as he rummaged through a stack of money that was in the console.

"Besides your water, you want anything else out the store, boo?"

"Some fruit chews will be fine." I reached into the back seat for my purse to give him a couple of dollars to grant my request.

He gave me a deadly stare, locking eyes with me as he continued counting his money, not missing a beat or looking down at his hands.

"Baby girl, when you're with me, everything is all good. Ok, boo? I mean *everything*. And what flavor candy you want?"

"Wild berry?" We both agreed and blushed in unison.

"Be right back, babe." I watched him in the passenger mirror as his sexy ass strutted across the parking lot behind me, speaking to a couple of homeboys on the way. I powered my cell completely off and sat it in the cup holder beside me. Minutes later, Rashaan returned with the snacks.

"Here you go, boo. I bought a couple packs because those my favorite ones too, so save a nigga some." He laughed again, making my heart smile.

"I got you, boo. So, you gon' tell me where we're headed now? You know, just in case I have to call Benson and Stabler to rescue me."

"We just going to the boot really quick. I go back home all the time, so I can do that drive and come straight back with no problem."

"Louisiana? Ok, cool. Well, let me get my nap on while you work this wheel." I stretched my hands above my head before ripping open the candy and stuffing a piece into my mouth.

After the gas finished filling up, Rashaan replaced the pump on the cradle, wiped his hands with a washcloth, then we were back on the freeway jamming to the hottest R&B hits of the 90's while enjoying each other's company.

I could really get used to this kidnapped shit.

Chapter Twelve

Enzo

I shook my head as I walked around the apartment finding some shit to throw on. When a few minutes passed by and Shara hadn't joined me in the shower, I rinsed the soap off my body, and stepped out to wrap a towel around myself before walking through the house to look for her. I could tell that she was super pissed when she left because the apartment door was unlocked and slightly cracked open. I walked to the island in the kitchen to grab my phone, praying that she didn't crack my lock code and find any messages between Neiysha and I. The last thing I needed was for my bitch to find out I was cheating yet again.

When I called her a few minutes ago, I could've sworn that I heard her talking to a nigga, but I could've been tripping because my girl didn't do shit that. Yeah, I know I've cheated on her many times in the past, but I never thought that she would return the favor. I pulled on a pair of sweats and matching hoodie, grabbed my cell and keys and headed outside to my whip in the parking lot. I called O'Shara's phone again a couple times and was steady sent to voicemail.

I didn't need this fuck shit right now. We had been doing good. I had even stopped fucking with Neiysha unless it was about some bread. Shara's ass was always a good detective. Every time over the years when a nigga was fucking hoes, my sloppy ass got caught and had to beg like Keith Sweat and Johnny Gil to make her love me again. I vowed to never fuck over her again, but Neiysha showed a nigga a lil more attention in the bedroom that Shara didn't want to. I knew that it wouldn't be easy to not fuck Neiysha anymore, especially being that she hooked me up with this lil side gig. Lately she had just been keeping shit between us about business, so I was cool with that.

I hopped on the freeway and headed East to my girl's best friend's house. I knew that's where she was stashing out at. Shara stopped going by her mom's house when we got into it because her family would start to judge our relationship and look at me sideways every time she went and ran her mouth when things didn't go her way. The closer I got to Charaty's, the more I called Shara's line. I didn't give a fuck if I had to put her thick ass on the hood of my ride and bury my head deep in that fat ass pussy of hers outside in front of everybody. She was coming home with me tonight.

About twenty-five minutes later, I was pulling into Charaty's apartments. I parked my whip alongside the fence that said visitor's then sat there for a minute thinking about my next move. I didn't know how to explain to O'Shara about my side gig, and a part of me didn't want to tell her shit. Hell, if a nigga was bringing in enough dough to take care of her and the house, she should've been good. I was pissed at myself for leaving the evidence out for her to find, but a bigger part of me was glad that her nosey ass didn't touch my phone.

I scrolled my address book for Charaty's number and dialed it as I hopped out my whip and made my way down the sidewalk to her apartment. She sent me to voicemail, but that was what she usually did when me and her girl got into it. She always took Shara's side and I expected that. I continued walking to her apartment and knocked on the door. After waiting a couple minutes, I called Shara's line once again and got the voicemail for the final time that night. It seemed as if she had her phone off and didn't want to be bothered, so I decided to let her be.

I started to make my way down the sidewalk when I heard my name being called.

"Aye, Enzo, what's up?"

Turning to the familiar female voice, I wished it was my girl ready to run into my arms, but it was only her best friend. Charaty lightly jogged my way with a disturbed look on her face.

"Shara ain't here. She came by earlier but left awhile back. I tried calling her but got the voicemail twice."

"Oh, word?"

"Yeah, I told you this shit wouldn't work." She laughed, "I know my best friend. She thought we forgot her damn birthday. Hopefully she comes back in time tomorrow for her dinner."

"Yeah, I hope so too. I had something else special planned for her as well. But, a'ight, if she hits you up then let me know please."

"Will do. You be safe."

I nudged my head at her before making my way back down the sidewalk towards the parking lot. I didn't know if my eyes were playing tricks on me, or I just didn't see it at first because I was trying to get to Charaty's spot fast as fuck. Backed into a parking spot right in front of me was O'Shara's ride. I wasn't tripping when I thought I heard a nigga's voice in the background earlier. I went to my ride and sat inside for a few minutes, waiting to see if Shara would appear from her friend's apartment. After about twenty minutes of her not showing herself, I decided to go back to the crib.

Me: I don't know what kind of game y'all playing, but it's cool tho. I saw Shara's car parked outside ya crib when I left. Just let me know if she's coming tomorrow. If not, I need to let our families know ahead of time.

I looked down at my cell, waiting on her half ass response, but she never replied. I didn't have time for the bullshit they had going on for real. This wasn't the first time my girl had hid out at her friend's house when she didn't want to fuck with me. As I drove back home, I was tempted to call my girl, but I felt that shit would work out better if I just let her make the next move.

I touched my pocket feeling the small square box that held her blinged out engagement ring I finally had enough money to buy. I loved the fuck out of O'Shara, and even though all our days weren't sunny in the past, she is who I planned to expand a future with. As soon as I pulled into my designated parking spot at our apartment and killed the engine, Neiysha was blowing a nigga phone the fuck up. I exhaled and looked to the ceiling, not ready to feed into her bitchin' and whining. If it wasn't about bit'ness or money, I didn't have time to listen to shit. I ignored the call, jigged out my ride and made my way upstairs to my apartment. After taking a leak and washing my hands, I saw that Neiysha had sent multiple text messages.

"Fuck!" I shouted aloud.

The money I was getting making drops for her was more than good, but when you stopped fucking a bitch and tried to do business, that shit didn't mix at all. I opened the messages and my eyes widened, leaving me speechless.

Overtime: Hey, my kids came in town early. Can you take them to their Pop's house for me?

Overtime: Look, I'll pay you double gas money this time. Hit me back and let me know please.

Chapter Thirteen

Armis

"Hey, Uncle Ronnie! What's up?" I looked over my glasses and spoke to my favorite uncle who passed by my open room door as I swiftly moved my fingers across my game controller.

"Ok, baby. I'll be back before breakfast. It's some chicken wings on the stove. And if you need anything else, you know where to find it."

I nodded my head to my mother as she peeped in my room before heading out the door for her overnight shift at the hospital. After losing the last round of the game I was playing, I made my way to the kitchen and washed my hands to make myself something to eat.

"It's some rice in that pot too over there if you want some. Boy, yo' Mama could always fry the hell outta some damn chicken."

After putting a couple pieces of chicken and a heap of rice and gravy on my plate, I sat down at the kitchen table and started to get my grub on.

"So, how's that game coming along? Have you reached the final level yet?" Uncle Ronnie asked as he sat across from me at the table.

"It's going good, and I'm almost there. I'll probably make it later tonight when I get done here."

"Look, I'm going to go downtown and pick you up a copy of the new game that comes out tomorrow. My friend Reggie is coming over in a bit to play cards, so don't be up on that game system all night. I don't want your mama to kick both our asses." He tapped me on the shoulder before heading back to the living room.

My mother was a few years older than her brother. Ever since he came back from the military, she had taken him under her wing after their parents had passed. Some nights he would have a bad case of PTSD and his friend Reggie helped him out.

After I finished eating, I cleaned up behind myself and took a shower. By the time I got out, I could hear that my uncle's guests had arrived. I knew that their night would be full of loud conversation and arguing that was brought on by Uncle Ronnie's famous hooch. I got dressed, buried my clothes in the dirty hamper and slowly walked down the hallway.

"How you doing, Mr. Reggie." I spoke to my Uncle's friend.

"Hey there, Armis."

"Ok, I'm going to bed now, Uncle Ronnie. Goodnight."

"Goodnight," I told the men before going back down the hallway to my room.

I noticed a different appearance than usual in my uncle's friend, but that wasn't my damn business. When I got to my room, I played another round on my game system before dozing off to sleep.

***

"Nah, fuck this shit, Ronnie! I'm tired of being your late-night hype. I'm too damn pretty to be your secret or second option. You either accept me for who I am, or I'm done fucking you!" A man screeched in a high-pitched voice.

"It's- It's not that easy, ok. I-I'm not ashamed of you or us. I just don't want you to be targeted or hurt by the opinions of others."

"If you can bend me over and fuck me in a skirt, then you can walk by my side publicly while I dress as my true self, a woman!"

"Honey, look, please. Don't do this. Why are you so loud? You're gonna wake the whole damn neighborhood," Ronnie pleaded.

I stood with my door cracked and listened to them go back and forth.

"Fuck you and this damn neighborhood. This the same neighborhood that labels yo' ass a crazy motherfucker after going to fight for your country. The least they could give you is some damn respect for the blood, sweat and tears we put up for their judgmental asses. I'm gone. Since you're so embarrassed of my feminine ass, you can watch me twirl out this damn door! It ain't the 80's no more motherfucker. I ain't hiding who I am for no damn body!"

I crept down the hallway and watched as the woman walked around the living room gathering her belongings.

"Armis, go back to bed, nephew. The sun will be up in a bit and we'll be on our way to get your game, ok."

Uncle Ronnie wrapped his strong arm around my shoulder and led me back to my bedroom.

"Yeah, nephew, go back to bed, so you won't see the truth that your uncle is fucking punks," the woman grunted as her thick heels clacked on the wooden floors.

I couldn't see her face, but she sounded just like my uncle's friend, Mr. Reg. I did as I was told and went back to my room. Being only a pre-teen at the time, my mind wondered about certain things, but I wouldn't dare ask about them.

I've been caught snooping in my Uncle's room before and found dirty magazines of women who looked like women on the outside but shared the same things between their legs as me.

The next morning, my uncle took me downtown as promised to get my new video game.

"How about some pancakes? Let's go down to the diner to get some."

We found an empty booth and sat down. When the server came to take our order, my Uncle was speechless as he stared at the TV screen.

"Earlier this morning around five a.m., local police responded to a phone call regarding an altercation outside of a bar. When law enforcement arrived on the scene, they found a victim that had been fatally stabbed. Witnesses identified the victim as this man, Reginald Goldberg. It is unclear what exactly caused the confrontation and the assault on Mr. Goldberg. This part of town is known to be where many transgender women hang out...."

"Dead! He's dead? Noooo. If I would've just let him stay at the house, this wouldn't have happened." Uncle Ronnie jumped to his feet, pulling me behind him as we exited the restaurant.

I sat back on the couch next to Karmyn with my arm wrapped around her. I could tell that she was different when we met that night at the club. When I would look at my uncle's dirty magazines of those different women, it didn't disgust me or turn me away. It turned me on. I never said anything to anyone about my secret fetish because I didn't want to be judged as my Uncle Ronnie was. It was hard watching him over the years fight with himself as he grieved about his one true love and who he really was. Up until this day, I had fought back the continuous urges I felt inside. I tried going to the Army to help toughen up my wicked desires. I even thought that me fucking multiple bitches at a time would cure me from my secret. When Charaty told me it was a possibility Ahmani could be mine, I felt that was the exact thing I needed to help me drown out the undisclosed truth about me. I'm not sure what it was, but I became an abusive beast when I had sex with women. I felt like they knew my secret truth and could see through me.

I looked down at my cell and saw the multiple missed calls and texts from Charaty. That bitch didn't really give a fuck about me. She never asked how my day was or how I felt. All she wanted was dick. That's the only time she would shut her fucking mouth up, when I was fucking her.

Baby Mama: Oh, so you are looking out these blinds but can't answer my calls, huh?

Baby Mama: It's cool. Fuck you. You won't ever see me or the baby ever again.

"Is everything ok, boo?" Karmyn asked sleepily as she curled up next to me.

"I'm. I'm not too sure. It's my baby mama-"

"Wait. You have a child?" She sat up and asked with wide eyes. "Not that it's a problem, you just never mentioned it."

"Well, because I'm not sure how far this thing will go. And I'm also not sure if the baby is mine."

"Ok, ok, one of those," she laughed. "It's ok, baby, I completely understand. I mean, you a fine ass nigga, so I assumed you had a girl or family back at home. Don't worry. I'm used to being on the side."

Even though she spoke with confidence, I could tell that she was bothered by her own words. If I were to ever come out of my trapped feelings, I would be open to the world. I wouldn't be a sellout like my uncle and let someone who loved me for my true self feel that I had to hide my feelings for them because of the way the world felt.

"No, love. I'm single. But there's this chick I was fucking with off and on for a couple of years outside of her relationship that told me I could be a possible father to her young child. We haven't taken any DNA tests yet, and I'm not even sure if her nigga knows he's a possibility as well, but I wouldn't lie to you about this. I want us to get to know each other here first," I said, placing my index finger on her temple then her heart. "And here before we even go down any other paths, you've been nothing but honest with me ,and I refuse to lie to you. What I'm telling you is the truth. I look out for her lil one and we haven't fucked around like that in a couple weeks. After we get this DNA test, it'll let me know where to go from there."

"It's ok, Armis, I understand." She stood and walked to the entrance door of her apartment.

"Thanks for the food and thanks for coming by tonight. Just get at me when you handle your business with your lil one, a'ight?"

I pursed my lips and shook my head. I didn't want Karmyn to think I was being dishonest, but I didn't want to pressure her to fuck with me either. I stood, walked to the door, placed a kiss on her cheek and dipped. I prayed that when I got home, Charaty's crazy ass wasn't outside my door with that trip shit.

Chapter Fourteen

Neiysha

"Ugh!" I grunted as I paced back and forth in my bedroom.

Enzo had really been a bitch made nigga lately. Sometimes I regretted helping his ass out being that he wasn't even fucking with me like that anymore. Call me crazy, but I really thought in my mind that I could have him all to myself. Shit, I knew for a fact that I treated him better than that haunted womb having bitch he went home to nightly.

"Yeah. What's up?" I answered my cell without letting it ring completely. "Hello!?" I shouted again, not hiding my agitation.

"Damn, what the fuck is up with you?" Thugga's deep voice came through the speaker on my phone.

"Nothing, cuz. What's up?"

"I'm trying to see if you got up witcha boy yet? I really need that taken care of for me tonight if possible."

I rolled my eyes and sucked my damn teeth. This nigga was starting to get on my got damn nerves. Until my kinfolk made it back to Texas this go round, he wasn't even fucking with me like that. Sometimes I felt that his two-strike ass was just using me to keep his dirty hands clean.

"Look, Rashaan, the nigga ain't even hit me back yet. I'm waiting on his response. Shit, I told him what you said but-"

I stopped my words and exhaled, thinking about my next words before they escaped my mouth. This nigga was in dire need of his shit getting delivered so I knew he would pay me whatever I asked for without a negotiation.

"Look, I rapped with him earlier and he said that he out of pocket right now."

"Ahh, shit, for real fam? Ok, that's cool then. I'll work something out."

"But he'll be back this way around midnight and he can do it, but he's gonna need two."

"Huh, what?" That nigga played like he couldn't fucking hear my ass.

"Two!" I shouted sarcastically with my lips on my speaker.

"Damn, a'ight then, Neiysha. And you better take yours off that two too."

"Oh, you know I will."

Before we ended the call, I could hear a female's voice in the background, but that wasn't the business that paid me. Shit, I was used to my big cousin being somewhere ducked off tricking with some pussy. If the bitch was smart, she better had made sure that nigga put them ends on the dresser first.

Chapter Fifteen

Shara

That night in the boot…

I stood in the large window that overlooked the pool and lounge area watching the guests and their families enjoy themselves. I heard the flowing water cease in the bathroom just a few feet away from me which let me know that Rashaan was done showering. Tightening the belt on my soft, terry cloth robe, I tried to hide the fact that I was becoming hot and bothered. I wasn't sure if it was because of the Queen treatment I was receiving from my newfound friend, or the sight of his caramel colored, impeccably carved body. Enzo had a nice shape himself, but when you had a sour attitude that went along with a sexy body, people tended to look over that.

I could see Raashan's reflection through the window as he crept up behind me.

"What's up, boo? You hungry?"

He asked, wrapping his strong arms around my waist. Through the towel, his bulky manhood rubbed against the back of my thighs, making my pussy drip. Fuck yeah, I was hungry, hungry for his dick! I thought to myself, hoping he couldn't hear my wicked thoughts about his sexy ass.

"What's wrong, Shara, you good, ma?" He asked again, turning me from the window to face him.

As soon as our eyes met, I held onto his shoulders to lift myself and straddle his waist with my thick thighs. I wasn't sure what he had in his hands at the moment, but I heard it hit the floor. I sucked his full, pink lips into my wet mouth and wrestled my pulsating tongue against his. The way his masculine hands massaged all over my ass let me know that he craved me as I did him.

"Mmmn..." I moaned as he walked me over to the bed, ready and willing to grant my request.

He laid on top of me, making my chest heave up and down at a fast pace as he pecked on the top of my breasts. I ripped my robe open, begging him to stop teasing me by shoving my erect nipple into his mouth. He locked eyes with me as he nursed on one breast nipple and squeezed the other between his fingers, turning me on even more. I placed my trembling hands on his bare chest and pushed him off me, then sat up to remove my bathrobe and threw it on the floor. His eyes widened like young Quincy McCall when he saw Monica naked for the first time in the movie Love & Basketball. A wide smile of confidence spread across my face. I pulled him by his ears until met his face with mine. Taking his mouth into my trembling lips, made my pussy drip.

"You sure you want this, baby?" He asked, hesitating to give me what I desperately needed, making sure it's what I truly wanted at the time.

"I need it. I need you now!" I demanded, reaching down to grab his hard dick that was poking against my thighs.

I took no time sliding him inside me. We both moaned in satisfaction then started to get into it with each other. He was gentle and sensual, yet seductive. I knew that I had been with Enzo and only Enzo all my life, but we've never made love. For the first time in my life, I was doing something deeper than fucking.

I sat at my desk in a dreamy daze thinking about the fun-filled weekend I'd had with Rashaan. The way that nigga had me bent over and sliding off the mattress had a bitch thinking he invented fucking. I wasn't sure if I enjoyed that dick so much because it was my lil hot pussy's first time with someone else outside of my lengthy relationship. Or because Rashaan's thug's lovin' was so damn good to me that he secretly had me wanting to pop out a few of his good hair having babies and be a stay at home wife forever. He didn't pressure me into anything, I wanted it. Hell, I needed every inch of that hood dick he buried into my quivering juice box.

Beep! Beep!

My headset alerted me that I had another customer calling in. I snapped out of my thoughts and got back to business.

"Sterling Inc, this is Shara here. How may I help you today?"

"Yes, ma'am. I'm calling to add a package to my TV. Hello, young lady?'

I rolled my eyes at the raspy voice having old bat. Lil freaky ass was calling in to add a porn package so she could play with her old, wrinkled ass pussy that probably spit out dust when she came.

"No problem, Mrs. Harris. I can get that added for you in just a jiffy."

"No, baby, it's not Mrs., I'm not married anymore. Wilfred went on to glory about three years ago. If he was still here, I would be making one of these love movies not watching one." She laughed, making me queasy.

I took out my notepad and jotted down her credit card info. I know I told myself that I would stop this shit with Karmyn, but getting the extra money was so addicting.

Kay: Hey, when you finish this call, come to my station please.

An instant message flashed across my computer screen. After ending the call with my last customer, Ms. Old and freaky, I signed out my account, crumbled up my paper of evidence and tucked it into the pocket of my slacks.

I absolutely hated working with females. Our supervisor Kay was a bitch and wore that title faithfully. I didn't even like asking the bitch for help when I needed it because she always had a stank look on her face when I did. I took my time walking to her desk, praying that she hadn't found out about my lil side hustle.

"Hey, O'Shara. How are you today?"

"I'm doing fine, and you?" I responded, biting my inside jaw to ease my nervousness.

"Doing good. Doing good," she nodded as she searched through her computer for something.

I watched her as she grabbed a pen and notepad and jotted down info. Before she pulled the paper from the pad and passed it to me, she completely shocked me with her words.

"Congratulations! You've been chosen for an interview for the new coach's position." She smiled, completely stunning me.

I swallowed the large lump in my throat and exhaled. "Wow! Me, really?"

"Yes, it's this Wednesday at 9 a.m. Good luck again, you got this."

"Ok, thanks."

I read over the information on the paper my supervisor had just given me and turned to go back to my desk. As soon as I got ready to log on to my computer to finish out the hour I had left in my shift, I received another instant message from my supervisor.

Kay: The day is done, go ahead and leave a few minutes early. Go celebrate your good news, ill clock you out at your regular time. It's fine.

Me: Ok, thanks again.

I closed out my station, grabbed my belongings and made my way out the building. Karmyn texted me earlier to meet her at Reno's for drinks again. I had debated my whole shift if I wanted to go or not. Being that I had been M.I.A. all weekend and ignoring everyone's calls, I'm sure that whenever I did go back to me and Enzo's crib, an argument was waiting for me. I made it to the parking garage and pulled out my cell to text my homegirl with one hand while starting my engine with the other.

Me: Hey boo. I left work a little early, so I'll be heading to the spot now.

Karmyn: Ok, bitch. I just pulled up, so I'll be here waiting on you.

Twenty minutes later, I pulled into the parking lot of the bar.

Rashaan: How's your day going ,beautiful? Thanks for a wonderful weekend. I can't wait to see you again.

As I strutted across the parking lot, I gloated at the text message. The weekend of love making we shared with one another was beautiful indeed.

Me: No. Thank you. You treated me like a Queen. I loved every moment of it.

Rashaan: Just got to give respect when it's due. Hit me up later tonight, maybe we can have dinner or something.

Me: Ok, love, I will.

I loved the way this man was making me feel. Shit, he treated me so fucking good that a bitch completely forgot that I was in a whole relationship.

"Shara, what's up, boo?" Karmyn greeted me with a tight embrace.

"Hey, boo. What you been up to?"

"How was your diva day girl?"

"Girl, shit, it was just another day," I lied. "Can you believe that my man and supposed to be best friend forgot all about it?"

"Say what, bitch? Uh uh, I need some shots for this tea session!"

She signaled over to the bartender and ordered us a round of Fireball shots. Before the glass hit the bar in front of her, she took two of them straight to the head.

"Yes, girl. I just drove to the northside, got me a hotel room, pigged out on room service, caught up on all my shows and turned my phone on do not disturb. I haven't even been home yet. Hell, I don't even know if I want to go for real though."

Karmyn's eyes widened in awe. She rested her elbows on the bar, staring at me with piercing eyes as if she could read through my lying ass.

"I ain't even mad at you, boo, for real. You gotta know your worth. If you don't, who else will? Shit, what you should've done was have you a nice, hard piece of dick laying up next to you, oiled up and bucket naked." She burst out laughing, knocking me out of my trance about the awesome weekend I had.

"Any who, boo, what's been up with you? I know you got some tea too, heaux." I quickly put the spotlight on her ass.

"Girl, I got man problems. Real man problems. Shit, my trade wont respect the fact that I'm going to chop my dick off. And this new nigga I'm dealing with ain't used to a woman like me and act like he's scared to fuck. Bitch, I am in heat! And I need to fuck something for real, for real. Shit, I ain't been fucked good in so long, I forgot how to moan. I'ma fuck around and bark while that nigga buried deep inside me and scare the fuck outta both of us," she spoke freely, making the bartender shake her head as she brought the next round of shots.

"Girl, yo' ass is crazy! But what's up with your new boo, why you think he acting like that? Maybe all that ass is too much for him to handle, girl." I pumped her head up with a nice compliment and gently poked her manmade derrière that instantly bounced back at me in thanks.

"No, it's not that. I think that he's not ready to come out yet. See, the hardest part about being gay is accepting your true self. You have to do that before anyone else will accept you. I don't think he's trapped in the closet completely. Like, he knows this lifestyle is what he wants, but that nigga surely is peeking out that motherfucker." I almost fell off the barstool laughing at Karmyn's crazy ass. I wish I had the courage to be as blunt and as free as she was in her true self.

"He do got a big dick though. Shit, that's something I am going to have fun with. I'm glad it ain't small. Shit, my lips too big for smedium ass dicks. That's like giving a whale a Tic-Tac, I can't suck that lil ass shit! See, girl, look." She pulled out her cell and showed me pics her boo sent of his heavenly hung, well-endowed piece.

"Umm, don't look too hard, your mouth look like it's watering and shit."

"Girl, no thanks. Shit, sometimes I don't even want the nigga I got," I drunkenly admitted and swallowed the truth that just came out my lips with another shot. "So, what's his story? Why is he hiding behind is truth? Baby mama? Wife?" I asked, enjoying the fuck out of the tea session that was causing me not to focus on my life at the moment.

"He says he has a possible child; he was upfront and honest about that. But the chick seems crazy though. Every time we're chilling when he comes over, that bitch be blowing up his cell. I don't know who she is or where she's from, but I told him I don't do the drama. Shit, it's enough drama being in the gay world as a transwoman. He's fine as fuck though. Girl, that sweet, caramel, sun-kissed skin, and those wishbone shaped legs. I should've known he was working with a monster."

"Damn, he must really be fine to be packing around that hammmm. Let me see a picture of your, boo."

"Here, girl, let me pull up his page real quick." She passed me her phone and I almost choked on my yak looking at the pictures of the familiar face my lifetime best friend Charaty was madly in love with.

"What's wrong, boo? Why you looking at him like that, you know him or something?"

I shook my head. "Nah, he looked familiar a lil, but I don't know him., I lied quicker than a two-dollar hoe to her pimp and quickly passed the cell back to Karmyn.

"Yeah, girl, that's my lil friend or whatever." She kept going on about Armis' tired, trifling ass while I tried my best to tune her out. Being that Charaty was my best friend, I wanted to ignore the scoop. But finding out the nigga she was crazy as hell over was undercover, made me want to listen.

Enzo: Baby, look... I'm sorry, ok? Come home tonight please? I'll rub and suck on them pretty ass toes.

I decided not to respond back. I was gone be home, but when I got good and damn ready. I was mad at myself now for turning my phone off do not disturb. Sometimes it seemed the only time Enzo gave a fuck about me being pissed about some fuck shit he did is when I gave him the silent treatment. Niggas couldn't take that shit, but they could definitely dish it out.

"Girl, speak of the devil, look who's calling now." Karmyn flashed her phone screen that showed an incoming call from Armis.

"Well, girl, you go ahead and take care of that. I'm tired and have to get ready for my interview I texted you about." I pulled two twenty-dollar bills from my purse, sat them on the bar and tapped my friend on the shoulder before making my way out as she answered her phone.

"Hey, text me that new info you got today, girl, and be safe," Karmyn called over her shoulder as I walked out the door.

I ignored her because after the good news I received today, I wasn't sure if I would be working my lil side hustle with Karmyn anymore.

***

The warm water felt soothing to my skin as it sprayed down on me. I tilted my head back and let the wetness flow all over my natural curls I sometimes hated showing. The strong Eucalyptus mint scent opened my nostrils, relaxing my body on impact. I closed my eyes and imagined I was ducked off in the boot again. All I could do was wrap my arms around myself and smile. I finished washing my body, shut the water off and stepped out onto a towel.

After wrapping my hair and body with warm towels, I treaded down the short hallway that led to the kitchen to feed my growling tummy, courtesy of happy hour. Reaching into the fridge, I could see a large box. I figured that maybe it was some leftover take-out being that I hadn't been home in a couple days, so Enzo had to fend for himself.

I pulled the large box out and sat it on the counter. Looking through the clear window on the cake box and reading the words, *"Happy Birthday Baby"*, shocked the shit out of me. I looked at the price sticker and date on the box. I felt like a dumbass seeing that it was purchased on my birthday. I really thought that Enzo had forgot about my special day. I could hear keys in the door and soon, my eyes filled with tears.

"Shara, baby, I—" Enzo started, and I cut him off.

Running into his arms, I buried my face into his chest. I would never tell it, but I really felt like shit about what I did.

"Stop, baby, don't cry. I would never forget your birthday, boo. How could I? You mean everything to me."

Enzo took my hand and led me to our bedroom. Gently lying me on the bed and stripping my clothes away, Enzo took no time swallowing my flesh into his soul. As I laid there watching his head bop up and down in between my legs, all I could think about was my lust-filled weekend with my side boo. A part of me wanted to continue to love Enzo, then the other part of me wanted to know more about Rashaan.

I pushed out the thoughts of my soon to be ex and thought about how I was treated like a queen for my birthday. I grinded on Enzo's face, pretending it was my side nigga's. With my eyes closed, I had flash backs of Rashaan's monster dick going in and out of my gushy goodness.

"Aaahhh, oohhh, fuck!" I screamed before biting my lip to stop me from calling that nigga the wrong fucking name.

After making his face and nose look like a glazed donut, I watched him jump up thinking he was getting some pussy and stopped him.

"No, wait, I promised Charaty that I would meet her for dinner. She told me about the dinner y'all had planned for my birthday and said she wanted to make it up to me tonight. I promise to rock your world when I get back." I placed a sweet kiss on Enzo's lips, hopped off the bed and ran to the bathroom to shower, making sure I grabbed my cell phone on the way.

I received a couple texts over the days I was M.I.A. from my best friend letting me know about the dinner they had planned. I decided that I would make that up to her another time. Tonight was all about me and Rashaan. I needed to let him know about the situation I had at home.

"Damn, baby, ok." I heard Enzo say as I ran off.

I made sure to lock the door, so his worrisome ass wouldn't come barging into my business. I started the shower and pulled out my cell to text my boo to see where he wanted to meet. I had to make sure it was on the other side of town and nowhere near anyone I knew if I wanted this love affair to last. I had decided that tonight I would talk to Rashaan about Enzo's tired ass, but I hoped that it would push him away eternally.

Chapter Sixteen

Armis

Charaty: So, you gon' just keep ignoring me, huh?

Charaty: Fuck you! Me or my daughter don't need yo' dumb ass.

I silenced my phone and took a deep breath before looking in my review mirror at the lights on the sign of the building. For years I was tormented by my mother for my feminine tendencies. She blamed my late uncle for the reason I had a twist in my walk and sass sometimes when I spoke. I tried my best to hide the feminine tendencies that hid inside of my soul. When the family found out about my Uncle's secret, they automatically labeled me as being every single derogatory name known to man that offends the gay world. The bitch wasn't complaining when her brother would take on her parental responsibilities while she was out tricking with married men nightly.

I checked the time on my cell again seeing another missed message from my supposed to be baby mama.

Charaty: Look, I'm so sorry daddy. I just miss you so much. Look, baby girl going with her dad for the weekend, come over and lay up with me.

I blocked Charaty's number and jigged out my ride. All that dickmatized bitch cared about was dick. Over half the time I went by her crib, baby girl would be sitting in the corner playing by herself or had some kind of electronic device glued to her hand while her tired ass mama was pretending to be studying.

Charaty was an unemployed student. She got a couple dollars from me a month, and I was sure that nigga Samad took care of her and that damn baby. So, I was confused to why Ahmani wasn't potty trained. Shit, Charaty went to school online. It was no excuse to why she was a sorry ass mother. Sometimes I hated her because she reminded me of my sorry ass mama. She was so worried about me wanting to fuck with other bitches, but I wasn't even sure if I wanted her tired ass. I was trapped between who I really was and who I was portraying. I only kept Charaty along all these years to hide the fact that I was secretly attracted to men.

I walked slowly inside the building. Smelling the fresh cigar smoke and stench of sweaty bodies slammed against my face. I spoke to the wide shoulder bouncer who knew me as a weekly regular.

"What's up, dog?" The manager dapped me up. "Your girl just got here, she's in the back waiting on you."

I walked to the bar first and ordered a couple strong shots of cognac. After taking them to my head, I walked down the long, dark hallway and stopped at door H. Even though I had been here so many times before, tonight felt different. Tonight, I felt like I would finally give in to my sexual desires. I took a deep breath before turning the knob and treaded in. Sitting in the lone chair that sat in front of the glass window, my legs shook as I waited impatiently to see my beauty.

Chapter Seventeen

Enzo

Me: Ok, baby. I'll be there as soon as I get off

Me: Is everything good, boo? How did your interview go?

When O'Shara didn't text me right back, I felt something was wrong. Then when my phone vibrated from an incoming text, I relaxed a bit.

O'Shara: Everything is fine, just wanted to talk about our future, that's all. And the interview went well. I start my coach training next week.

Me: Ok cool boo. Well I'm headed back to the warehouse, just finished my route. I'll see you when you make it home, boo.

O'Shara: Ok, baby.

Supe: Aye, when you come in for the day, I need to rap witcha'. Come to my office please.

I looked down at my phone in disgust and shook my head. I hated that Bobby's ass was working today. He was one of those supervisors that liked to watch over your every move and waited for you to fuck up so he could bitch about it. I didn't even respond back to his text because I'll admit that nigga had me bothered a bit. I wasn't for his bullshit and bitchin' today. I just wanted to clock out. go home to my gal and relax to enjoy my off days.

I pulled into the warehouse and killed the engine after parking my work truck. Making sure I grabbed my backpack and keys, I made my way to Bobby's office as he requested.

"Man, this some fucked up shit, bruh!" My coworker, Donnie, shouted as he left Bobby's office, almost slamming the door behind him.

"What's up, dog? What happened?" I asked, wanting to know what the fuck was happening. I looked behind me in the warehouse and saw a couple of my other coworkers were pissed as fuck too.

"Enzo Thomas! You're next. step in please and close the door behind you." Bobby locked eyes with me through the blinds of his office window.

With shaky legs, I stepped into the small room and did as I was told. Taking a seat in the wobbly metal chair that sat in front of the desk, I exhaled deeply and swallowed the large lump that sat my throat.

"How are you doing today?" Bobby asked nonchalantly like I didn't just witness some fucked up shit going on around that bitch.

"I'm straight, Bobby, what's going on though?" I extended my arm his way to ease him up to getting to the fucking point.

"Ok, Mr. Cocky, there's no need for the small talk then. Let me just come out and give you the news."

"Let's get it." I placed my elbows on my knees and scooted to the edge of the chair to hear him out loud and clear.

"Well, there's no easy way to say this, but our company has been bought out by a new shipping service. They've let us know that they are choosing to keep only a few of our old employees. They've given us a list of who they want to keep and those individuals will have to interview for their current position or a higher-level position with the new company-" he started.

"Wait, so basically you're telling me that most of us that's been here for years slaving our asses off are out of a job?"

"That's the way it is. And I can understand just how frustrating this is. But I have good news for you, Mr. Thomas. You are one of the chosen few that can be moved to the new company. Well, if you can complete and pass an extended background check and hair follicle." He smiled through his cracked-up ass teeth. "I have some paperwork for you. Take this down to the medical clinic on Howard by 6:30 this evening to complete. After your results come back, you will have three days of paid training under the new company before you can start under them. Congratulations and good luck," he added sarcastically.

I nodded and grabbed the paperwork he handed to me. Remembering the written hurt all over my coworkers' before me faces, I decided to quickly fold up the paperwork and slid it into my work shorts. My heart almost dropped when Bobby said I had to pass a hair follicle and extended background check. My background would be straight thanks to my girl busting her ass off at work years ago to help me get it expunged by this expensive ass lawyer, but the hair follicle on the other hand had me shook. I knew I wasn't passing that shit no matter how hard I tried. I'd be a damn fool to waste my time and this new company's money going to that damn clinic.

"A'ight, thanks, man."

I jumped up from the seat, opened the door and hiked it to the employee parking lot. As soon as I slid into the driver's seat of my whip, there came Donnie's ass knocking on my passenger window. I popped the locks and told him to hop in.

"Man, dawg, my baby mama gon' kill my ass, nigga. I just got this motherfucking job not even six months ago and here they come with this out the blue ass bullshit." He pulled a fat ass blunt from his shirt pocket and started to light that bitch up.

"Yeah, it's fucked up for real. Shit, I don't know what the fuck I'ma tell O'Shara's crazy ass. They wrong though. A nigga been here for a lil minute and they on this sleazy shit. But fuck it, dawg, I ain't even trying to go back and forth. I'ma just finish these last couple weeks strong and let life figure this shit out."

"Shit, at least you get a couple more checks. That hoe told me my last day was today," Donnie revealed, making me cough after I hit his weed.

"Damn, dog, for real though?"

"Man, hell yeah, my nigga. Talking 'bout I been clocking in late and shit and a few of the customers accused me of not delivering their packages."

I sat back and listened to this nigga run his mouth after passing the square back. Most of the niggas at my job gossiped just like lil bitches, but it did intrigue a nigga slightly to hear this shit from the horse's mouth. I knew that nigga was stealing though. Donnie was cool as fuck, but he looked like a grimy ass nigga. He was from the slums of the city, and all then slummy ass niggas had a bad rep.

"Look, I'ma holla at you, Donnie Boy. I gotta figure out how I'ma break this news to my girl. If you hear about something, shit, hit me up."

"A'ight, bet." We slapped hands and he exited my whip as soon as his girl pulled up bitchin'.

"I'm glad I don't have those problems," I said to myself as I backed out my parking space. I know I had just told my gal I wouldn't be working late tonight but shit, now I had to see what I was going to do about bringing some kind of money into our home. After riding on the freeway in a blank trance for about 30 minutes, I snapped out of my thoughts and took the next exit. Traveling down the sandy gravel gave me plenty of time to think about my next move.

I'd fucked up big time and couldn't fault anyone but myself. A couple months back when I started running dope for this Thugga nigga, one of the packs busted during transport. That shit was all over my work truck and shit so I tried my best to clean it up and pack it back the best I could. During clean up, I was curious if this nigga was really moving some heat, or just had me risking my job and freedom over some bullshit. So, my dumbass scooped some dust up and pressed it on my tongue. That shit was so potent, it had a nigga mouth dumb numb for days.

Before when I was with my side bitch, she would put some of that shit on my dick and suck it off, but I'd never tried it or wanted too. It had to be some of the same shit her kinfolk had because that shit was fiya. After tasting some out of the busted pack, I start saving some dust for me to enjoy on my stressful days. I noticed myself getting greedy with the shit, but it was too late, I was already hooked. If I would've known that bitch ass job was gon' pull that move, I would've never got involved with the shit.

So, now I'm fucked. I stopped delivering for that Thugga nigga and I lost my job. I didn't want too, but I needed to pull up on Neiysha to see if her fam needed me to move shit for him again. I had to do something because telling O'Shara the truth at a time like this wasn't an option.I looked up and saw that I was about three blocks away from Neiysha's complex. I didn't want to pull a female move and just pop up being that we hadn't communicated in a minute, but outta respect for her and her crib, I called as I backed into my usual parking space.

As expected, she sent me to voicemail with the quickness, so I started to text her some fly shit. She quickly hit me back before I could press send.

"Aye, what's up, boo?" I tried to butter her up.

"Whatever, Enzy, what's up, fool?"

"Oh really, that's how you doing a nigga?"

"Dude, what you want? You know you don't fuck with me. Man, hold up, somebody at my door."

"Shit, that's me, open up."

I hopped out my whip and made it down the sidewalk I'd frequented so many times while she was running her mouth. On the way up the stairs, I saw her downstairs neighbor peeking their nosey ass out the door. It seemed like as soon as they saw my face, they hid behind the door and closed it. Neiysha snatched the door open and looked me up and down in disgust.

"Damn, baby, that's how you greet a nigga? Man, come here." I pulled her into my embrace and tickled her hot spot on her neck with my tongue.

"Move, Enzo! Nigga, you know we don't fuck around like that for real." She tried pushing me away and that just made me want her more.

At this time, I wasn't caring about what I had at home. Shit, I wouldn't have shit left at home if she found out a nigga was broke again.

"I missed you, boo, and this how you act towards me?" I liked trying to work my way up to what I really came by for.

"Nah, nigga, you don't miss me. If you did then you wouldn't be away from me to miss me."

"Work just been having me stressed out, but I'm here now and I wanna make it up to you. Let's go to the bedroom."

I pulled her by her arms to the master bedroom. Neither of us wasted time stripping down to our birthday suits. O'Shara's pussy was a tad bit better than Neiysha's, but see, my hoe did shit I wasn't given at home. That bitch loved to eat my meat. Without hesitation, Neiysha dropped to her knees and buried her face in my crouch. My toes popped in my socks as she swallowed my shaft beneath her tonsils. She took her hand to the back of my thighs and slowly crept up my tight ass cheeks. She gently bounced her fingers down the crack of a nigga shit. I squeezed my shit so tight, Moses couldn't part them. It was then that I knew I had that bitch right where I needed her, back where she needed to be.

After massaging the kids up out my dick, Neiysha licked my shit dry and swallowed. That was another thing that turned me on that I didn't get at home. I knew she liked rough sex, so I snatched her up by her throat and threw her on the bed, demanding her to open her legs so I could finish her off.

"No, I can't. We can't. Look, I have to talk to you about something."

Fuck! I thought to myself. *Here this hoe go with this bullshit.*

"Really, at a time like this? You got a nigga standing up here ass naked and ashy, ready to run up in those guts and you on this trip shit? Man, pass me my drawls."

"Ok, fine. Since I ain't shit but a fuck to you, leave then. I don't care anymore, dude!" She threw a pillow at me then turned over on her stomach and started crying like a baby.

"All I ever did was care for you, try to help you out and look how you treat me!" She screamed.

"Look, I'm sorry, ok. Stop crying, man, come here." I pulled her my way and she climbed into my lap.

"Why do we keep doing this, huh? I'm tired of being your side bitch. Shit, sometimes I want to be held by you at nighttime too. Spend the night with me, please? Thugga coming by in the morning to bring some shit that he needs me to move. I wish you wouldn't have stopped making moves for him. Just because I dip in the shit from time to time doesn't mean I want to move it. Fuck that!"

Hearing that was music to my ears. "Well, another company is taking over my company so I'ma need to hook up with that nigga again--"

"Oh, so that's why you're over here? See, I knew it was something!" She smacked her lips and crossed her arms after jumping off me.

"Nah, boo. I really been missing you, well… us. And I wanted us to pick up where we left off."

"Ok, Enzo, whatever. But you still didn't answer my question."

"What's up, boo?" I kept my back to her as I gathered my clothes. She knew good and damn well I couldn't spend the night at her crib without pissing O'Shara off. "Let me see what I can do, babe. I'ma step out to my car real quick and see if I have a change of clothes in the car. I'll be right back." I heard her mumble something smart under her breath and paid it no mind.

I jigged down the steps and hiked to my ride. I didn't know just what to say to O'Shara, but if a night of letting Neiysha swallow my piece was going to get me back in good with her cousin, then I would have to do that until I could find another well-paying job. I rummaged through my whip and found a white tee and a pair of ballers I used to hoop in after work, laid that shit on my shoulder and made my way back down the sidewalk. When I got back up the stairs, I could hear laughter coming from the other side of Neiysha's door. At first, I thought she was just on speaker phone with one of her loud ass homegirls. When I walked back in the house, staring back at me as she sat across the table from Neiysha was the same neighbor I had seen earlier.

"Hey, babe. This is my homegirl, she lives downstairs. Karmyn, this is Enzo, my lil boo thang or whatever."

"Hi- How are you?" She asked, nervously looking like she had just saw a ghost. Well, I thought it was a woman, but clearly, I could tell the bitch could probably bench press two times my weight in the gym.

I spoke back, then made my way back to the bedroom. I knew Neiysha stayed on some freaky shit, but I wasn't down with that kind of threesome, so I hope she wasn't plotting nothing on me with her lil friend in there. I started the shower and undressed. Before hoping in, I texted a pic of my semi hard dick to Neiysha and told her to come meet me in the shower so she could get rid of her company. While I waited on her, I powered off my cell and decided to figure out the rest of my life in the morning.

Chapter Eighteen

Karmyn

Armis: I'll be there in about 30 mins, babe. Just made it to the house and hopped out the shower.

Me: Ok, boo.

Armis: Are you hungry? Or do you need me to pick up anything for you?

I started a steamy shower and sat down on the toilet while I contemplated on what to say back to Armis. I didn't know what to say to that nigga. He was cool, so I didn't want to push him away just yet. I sat my phone down and started busting down my cigar.

For the past couple months that we had been kicking it, we hadn't stepped one foot out of my apartment. All we did was talk, smoke, drink and chill. We would cuddle up from time to time, but we were never intimate beyond shoving our tongues down each other's throats and minimal groping. I was used to downlow niggas that knew exactly what they wanted and weren't afraid to bend me over and fuck this sweet boy pussy or let me swallow their unattended to dicks down my delicious throat. Armis was cool as fuck, but a bitch was in heat, and if he wasn't fucking tonight then he could step. I was craving sucking some dick. Shit, it had been so long that I almost forgot how to do it. But I'm sure it was like riding a bike and would come back to me like nothing.

Ever since I made the final decision that I would be going under the knife for my transition to my true self, my trade cut me off completely. So, if this Armis nigga wasn't tryna fuck something tonight, then he was gone have to move the hell around. Shit, I could go back to my old days on the track and get fucked and paid, but I graduated from those hoe tendencies.

Armis: I'm sorry boo. We will go out and about soon. I told you I'm still trying to figure this shit out.

Armis: Look if you don't want me to come, I'll head back home.

I rolled my eyes and stared at my phone before snatching it off the bathroom counter.

Me: I was sitting the trash outside. I don't know what I want yet. But I'm waiting on you, boo, so hurry but be safe.

Armis: I will, boo. You putting something sexy on for me?

I rolled my eyes, lit the tip of my square and inhaled deeply. I don't know why the fuck his simple ass was asking me that. Ain't like we was fucking, so why would I waste my sexy ass lingerie for his scared to fuck ass?

Me: I don't know. You'll have to see when you get here.

Armis: Ok, beautiful.

Me: See you soon.

"Shit!" I shouted to myself out loud.

I had just remembered that I did need to take the trash and sit it outside before the pickup crew came through. I walked to the kitchen, pulled the trash bag out and tied it before looking through the cabinet to find another bag. After getting the trash can situated, I walked to the front door of my apartment to sit the bag outside, hitting my fat ass blunt on the way.

I unlocked the door, stepped over the door ramp and almost lost my breath when I saw Enzo's piercing eyes staring at me as he stood across from me on Neiysha's steps. I sat the bag against the wall and rushed inside my apartment to close the door.

"Bitch, don't fucking try me!" He yelled as he forced his hands through the crack and made his way inside. I cowered behind my dining room table as he slammed the door with his foot.

Being a transwoman in the working trade, I learned early on how to protect myself. Motherfuckers sometimes thought that because I was a feminine man, I was also a scary bitch. But I had to fight all my life and was ready tonight if need be. I slowly reached under the dining room table for my blade I kept stashed just in case one of those undercover brothers that frequently came by to fuck me got out of line.

"You wanna be a bitch so bad, huh? How about I make you one! I'll beat your ass just like a bitch!" Enzo yelled before pouncing on me like an angry wild cat.

I palmed the blade just in time, hiding it between my closed fist and starting punching that bitch nigga in his face, splitting it open. At first, he didn't notice his face was busted open like a can of store-bought biscuits.

"Ahh!" I screamed when he hit me hard as fuck in my stomach and I dropped to my knees.

"Bitch nigga, you're the reason my girl fucking with that nigga! You're the reason she's cheating on me!" He wailed, now punching the large mirror that hung in my dining area.

I had only saw Enzo a couple times in passing and not once did I ever think that he was this type of monster. Both O'Shara and Neiysha spoke well of him, but I could tell by his body language that he was high as fuck. After being around my uncle Ronnie after the love of his life died, I'd seen the same monster plenty of times before.

"Fuck this shit! Fuck this shit!" He screamed until he was hoarse.

I stood back, blade still in my now bloody hands, ready to finish him off if I needed to. I watched him look down at his bloody hands and shake his head before he darted out the same way he came in. Slumping down against the wall, I cried thick, heavy tears. I had been in many fights and attacked in my life, but this was the scariest. I'm not sure what made Enzo come at me the way he did. I guess I was just the middleman in the crazy situation he and his girl created.

I felt so lost and alone, I didn't know what to do. I wasn't sure if going to the police would be a good idea. I just needed someone, anyone to be on my side. I wasn't perfect by far and this time, I had did absolutely nothing wrong.

"Karmyn? Baby! What the fuck happened in here?" Armis' voice and presence temporarily took me from my thoughts.

He walked over to me and squatted down where I sat.

"Baby, please talk to me. What happened? Let me at least take you to the emergency room," he begged, helping me off the floor.

"I--" I stumbled over my words. "I don't know if I should."

"What do you mean? You need too, babe, let's go."

"Armis, you're new to this world. It's different for us. They'll just assume it was another night on the track gone bad. They won't help me, they'll only judge me."

"Babe, listen to me. They'll have no choice. I'm taking you now so let's- wait." He stopped and paced back and forth.

"Do you know who did this to you?"

I froze in my steps and looked down at my blood-stained feet before shaking my head. I wouldn't dare reveal to anyone what Enzo did to me tonight.

"No. I don't know. I didn't even see the person's face that good. I stepped outside shortly after we got off the phone to sit the trash bag out and when I walked back in, the person forced themselves through the door as I tried to block it. I tried running away and we fought against the mirror, but I grabbed my blade from under the table and started swinging at his ass. I must've cut him. That explains all this blood and why he ran out."

"Ok, boo. I'm so sorry that this happened to you. It's all my fault. If I wouldn't have taken so long, this wouldn't have happened to you. I'm so sorry."

Even though I was busted up and bruised on the outside, my heart fluttered like butterflies in my chest as I felt loved and cared about truly for the first time in my life.

"I'm calling to see if a detective can come out to gather any evidence. Then I'll take you straight to the hospital, babe."

I nodded and sat down at the dining table, silently hating that I lied to this man. I wasn't sure if I would ever speak the truth about that night to anyone.

Chapter Nineteen

Charaty

Me: So, you can't answer your phone and I'm calling about Ahmani? Yeah, you over there with a fucking bitch. Don't make me come down that damn sidewalk, nigga!

I was pissed as fuck that Armis' had been dodging me for the past couple of weeks. I didn't know if he was just tired of dealing with me or he finally found someone.

"Wahhhh, wahhh! Mama!" Ahmani whined, getting on my damn nerves. I stomped out my bedroom to the kitchen to fill her sippy cup with Pedialyte.

She had been running a fever for the past two days. I avoided the hospital by alternating Tylenol and Motrin because I knew that's what they would tell me to do at the hospital. After filling her cup, I pulled her petite body in my arms and held her tightly. Placing my chin on her forehead, I could feel the heat that burned inside of her. Times like this as a mother, I hated. It was nothing worse in this world than not being able to take your child's pain away. Ahmani start whining again, making me cringe.

"Mommy ain't mad at you, baby girl. I'm just mad at the situation."

My cell rang with an incoming call from Samad. This is the last thing I needed at the moment. I hit the ignore button with the quickness. As I expected, his dumb ass video called. I know if I would've ignored him again, he would send his snitching ass son over to check on us.

"Damn, you don't see me calling, Charaty? How's my baby doing?"

"Samad, I don't need your fuck shit right now ok. I'm packing her bag up to take her to the urgent clinic."

I was tired of this nigga. I couldn't wait to finish school so I wouldn't have to depend on his controlling ass anymore. I loved the shit out of the beautiful blessing he gave me, but I was done being controlled. I hung up in his fucking face and powered by phone off.

Hoping off my bed and laying baby girl down with her cup, I jogged to the closet to pack her a bag to take with us to the clinic. I knew that Samad was blowing me up, but I decided that I would power my phone back on when I got to where we were going. I knew I had to move fast before he sent his instigating ass son to my crib.

I grabbed everything we needed and baby girl then made my way out the door, being sure to lock up behind me.

***

Almost twenty minutes later, we were pulling up to the urgent clinic across town. As I waited for the arm in the parking garage to rise, I powered on my cell so I could reach out to my bestie. Being that she was offered a supervisor position and now worked more hours at work, we hadn't spent much time together lately. At a time like this, I needed and wanted my best friend by me and Ahmani's side. Out of everyone, the possible fathers and even my own family, O'Shara never judged my parenting skills. She was always there for me when I needed her, even with my men problems never judging me.

I found a parking spot on the first level not too far from the entrance. Before getting out and grabbing baby girl's stroller from the trunk, I texted Shara to see if she could come comfort me and Ahmani.

Me: Hey boo. What's up?

Me: Girl I just pulled up to the urgent clinic with Mani, she's burning up.

Me: I was *hitting* you up to see if you could come sit up here with us.

I threw my cell in Ahmani's backpack and hopped out the driver's seat to grab my baby. I enjoyed the silence as I rode up the elevator. For the first time in two days, baby girl had finally dozed off for a few minutes. I prayed that when the nurses and doctors started messing with her, she didn't get cranky again. I just want my baby love to feel better. I hated when she was sick and there wasn't much I could do about it to make her feel comfortable.

After I filled out the paperwork to check Mani in, my phone start vibrating. I figured it was just Samad's worrisome ass again, so I took my sweet time fishing my phone out the bag. Surprisingly, it was O'Shara. I answered in a hurry, hoping that she was on her way to us.

"Hey, boo, what's up? How's my baby."

I looked over her gorgeous face that glowed in the screen as she locked eyes with me.

"Your Mani don't feel good," I responded in a baby voice and pouted before flipping the camera on the baby so she could see her.

"Aww, poor baby. What are they saying, Char?"

"Girl, we literally just got here so, I'm not sure what's the verdict yet, but I hope they give me something to make her feel better. She's been down for the past couple days. What are you up to though? I wasn't sure if you were off today, that's why I asked if you could come up here and keep me sane."

She tried to hide it, but I could tell that she was trying to hide something. It looked like she was lying in bed undressed, covered up with sheets. I didn't want to seem selfish knowing her and Enzo were on good terms this week for once, but he still was a hoe ass nigga in my book. Sometimes I wondered why Shara even dealt with his bummy ass. She talked shit about me and Armis, but at least that nigga kept a fucking job. He didn't spend hundreds of dollars on shoes every month then come up short for the rent monthly.

I felt in my heart that the right man would come for my dear friend one day; a husband. Someone she could spend her life with and finally have children by, but it wouldn't come until she dropped that trifling ass nigga she called bae.

"Who you on the phone with, bae?" An unfamiliar voice called out in her background. It could be because I was exhausted and tired from being up with my daughter the past couple days, but it didn't sound like the familiar voice I was used to. I brushed it off and decided to mind my business. If Shara had anything going on she wanted me to know about, she would've told me.

"You're gonna have to keep me posted with everything, babes, but I'm sorry I can't make it up there at this moment. I'm sure she'll be ok though. I have faith."

"Ok, boo, they're getting ready to call us to the back now, so I'll text you with any updates. Love you, bestie."

"I love y'all too, babes, kiss my Mani for me. I really hope she feels better."

We ended the call and I walk to the triage room as soon as I heard them call us.

"Mani baby. Here, drink some juice." I spoke softly to my daughter as she parted her weary eyes.

As the male nurse took his time taking her temperature and vitals, I noticed a tall slender woman with a man-made derriere emerge from behind the curtain and walk to the other side of the small makeshift room. I didn't notice that she could've been born a he until she started talking.

"Do I really have to file a police report? I mean, I don't want to, but my boyfriend wants me to. I fought that fucker back, so he got a piece of what he deserved," she started and I ear hustled like a motherfucker.

I could tell by the bloody bandages, and bruises to her face and neck that she was attacked by someone viciously.

"Ma'am, you can come down the hall this way, you'll be in room number three."

The nurse directed us to a bed for us to wait to see the doctor. They laid Mani down, and hooked her tiny arm up to an IV that was supposed to rehydrate her. After about thirty minutes, Ahmani dozed off again. When the nurse came in and asked if I needed anything, I asked if she could sit with my baby while I relieved myself in the ladies room. She agreed, and I was on my way down the hallway when

I ran into Samad. I gritted my teeth and kept walking like I didn't see his bitch ass until he blocked the doorway of the ladies room and stopped me.

"I've been calling you, Char. Why is my number blocked and where is my damn baby?"

"Move, Samad! I'm tired of your bullshit. Why should I call you just so you can insult my mothering skills? I'm surprised that you're even here to deal with her during one of her many sick days. You try to give me all this hell like I ain't shit because you can't control me. You wanna play daddy so bad? Then do something other than be a fucking ATM for the child you created. Move!"

I brushed past him and entered the ladies room, being sure to lock the door behind me. I lined the seat with tissue paper before sitting down and crying my eyes out. I'd had enough of being a pawn in everyone's else game. I was tired of being hurt and mistreated by people I thought loved me.

I finished my business, washed my hands and cleaned my face with cold, wet paper towels. I took a deep breath before exiting the ladies room and making my way back down the hallway to Ahmani. On the way there, I passed the same manly looking woman that was seated across from us in triage earlier. I decided to walk outside near the waiting area to get a breath of fresh air before I had to deal with my dumb ass baby daddy again and possibly catch a case.

"Hey, boo. You got a light?"

Ms. Transwoman asked me out the blue as she stood and waited on her ride.

"Oh, no, love, I don't smoke," I let her know.

"That's good. Shit, one of these days I'ma stop, but not today." She laughed. "It's cool, my dude went to get the car. I probably have one in the console. "That's your baby girl that's in there sick?" I nodded. "Hope she feels better, boo."

"Thanks so much."

"Hello? Damn, Armis, you don't see me standing out here. Look, I'm right here waving you down."

When that name rolled off her tongue and struck my ears, my hands began to shake. I burned with fury listening to her yell the usual name I screamed in my bedroom on occasion. *Calm down Char, calm down.* I spoke to myself, waiting for her dude to pull up, secretly hoping it wasn't my Armis. Minutes later, a candy black, two-door sports car whipped in the emergency room pick up driveway and I knew it was him. Armis pulled up and got out the car like a gentleman, opening the door for his boyfriend. Before she could get to the car, I jumped up from the bench I was sitting on and charged at Armis.

"You gay motherfucker, so you been dodging me and our child to lay up with some dick. You nasty bitch ass nigga!" I screamed as I attacked him with a nice ass two-piece combo.

"Ma'am! Ma'am! If you don't stop attacking him, I'll have to cuff you." The overweight rent a cop officer that was seated in the chair at the front desk earlier came to Armis' rescue.

"Hold up! Hold the fuck up. This the crazy baby mama you was telling me about? Oh no, baby, Karmyn don't break up happy homes, boo. You can have your nigga. I'll call an Uber." She walked off swinging her exotic weave, making me want to get on her ass too, but I instantly remembered she was born male and chances are she would probably kick my ass.

"Karmyn, Karmyn! Wait, baby, please! This hoe ain't shit to me, babe, and that ain't my fucking baby. She don't know who lil mama belong too."

Hearing those hurtful words come from the man I truly wanted and loved lips hurt me to the core. I snapped out of my trance and took my eyes off him as he followed his girlfriend down the sidewalk. To add insult to injury, when I turned around from the commotion, Samad stood just a few feet behind me with our daughter and her discharge papers in his hands with a perplexed look on his face.

Chapter Twenty

Enzo

Earlier that night…

I scrolled down the past text messages between me and O'Shara. I'd been missing the shit out of her lately. At first, I agreed that Shara and I needed some time apart. I was no longer pulling my weight in our home as a man. I figured she was fucking with another nigga though. I knew what all those "I'm working late" nights really meant. Shit, I had played the same game with her, so I couldn't fault her for giving me a taste of my own medicine.

When I went by the apartment, I was pissed that my girl was not there. I just knew she was somewhere with a nigga getting fucked. So, I went over to Neiysha's house hoping that she could suck all the pain out my dick and make me feel good. As soon as I jogged up the stairs that led up to her apartment, I got a text from Donnie's messy ass. I looked down at the pic he sent me, and it was O'Shara and some nigga boo'd up out in the open like she didn't give one fuck about me or what we had for all those years. At first, I couldn't see the dudes face that good, but Donnie's messy ass made sure he got a clearer picture that was up close the second time.

Donnie: Aye, ain't this yo' girl homie?

When I walked through the doorway, I figured Neiysha was in the shower waiting on me. As I stared at the picture of the dude hugged up with my woman, I knew he looked familiar. I walked to the bedroom and grabbed Neiysha's phone. Scrolling down her contact list, I stopped when I reached the name Big Cuz Thugga. Looking back and forth between our phones, I felt played like a motherfucker. This whole time Neiysha had been fucking me and her kinfolk was fucking my gal. If that wasn't some set up shit, then I don't know what the fuck was.

I slid my phone into my pocket and flew into a rage. I busted through the bathroom door and yanked that hoe out the tub. I didn't mean to kill the hoe, but I kept seeing O'Shara's face and all the pain I caused her as Neiysha's eyes rolled to the back of her dome. When I saw that she was no longer responsive, I left out the way I came, and that's when I spotted Karmyn stepping out of her apartment.

After I shattered the hanging mirror and saw the blood dripping from my hands, I ran out the apartment and jigged in my whip. I left out the complex driving like a mad person, now wondering where to go. I don't know what exactly forced me to attack my girl's neighbor, but I kind of feel that she was in the middle of all the bullshit that was going on in my fucked-up life.

Ain't no way in hell she was friends with both Neiysha and O'Shara and didn't let them know I was going back and forth between the two. If I wouldn't have snapped out the trance I was in when I did, I would've murked Karmyn's bitch ass just like I did Neiysha.

I gunned it to the freeway, hoping to escape before the police could catch up with me. I was mad at myself more than anything for allowing myself to lose the only woman that ever loved and cared about me.

Chapter Twenty-One

O'Shara

Three weeks prior…

I was tired of this shit with Enzo. I had already knew he lost his damn job because I followed him one day and he went everywhere but to the warehouse. I figured that he was probably fucking with another bitch too. I decided to let him dig a hole for himself, especially since he wasn't working anymore. Shit, I had no need for the nigga.

I had given my life and all to someone who didn't deserve a real woman like me. He finally came out and told me he had lost his job, but the reason why had me confused. I wasn't too sure if I believed the company just "let him go" because of a background I personally used all my savings for to fix. I told him that I felt we needed time apart. We had been together all our lives and I felt stuck. Nothing was progressing in a positive way; it was time to let it go.

"Damn, baby. Somebody blowing yo' shit the fuck up. Lemme find out it's that nigga wanting you to come back home."

I laughed at Rashaan's crazy ass and rolled off his chest to pick my phone up from the nightstand near my side of the bed. After Enzo had been staying out and not coming home recently, there's no reason for his bitch ass to be hitting my line. I had a new job position, a great man, and we were looking at homes. I'd be a damn fool to turn my back on this fairytale lifestyle to entertain his foolishness.

I grabbed my phone with sleep still in my eyes and saw that I had several missed calls from Charaty. My heart fluttered in my chest as I thought the worse. I prayed that everything with Ahmani was fine.

"Oh, my goodness. That was my best friend. I hope everything is ok with the baby."

"For real, boo? You want to ride by there?"

I sat up in the bed and called Charaty back on speaker.

She sent me to voicemail twice, so I called a third time and that's when I missed an incoming text from her.

Bestie: Oh, so now you're dodging my calls huh? Fuck you! Fake ass bitch! you knew Armis was fucking yo' gay ass coworker and didn't say shit.

Bestie: You probably hooked them up with yo' grimy ass!

Bestie: No wonder why that lil dick ass nigga cheat on yo' stupid fat ass!

"Wow, really?" I laughed. "This bitch really took it there, huh? Baby, look at this shit. So, this don't know who the fuck her baby daddy is, loose pussy ass hoe mad at me because my homegirl fucking her undercover side nigga. Look what this bitch sent to me." I passed my phone to my new boo and let him see the incoming messages from Charaty crazy ass.

"I thought that was your best friend, babe. Damn, what got her wildin' the fuck out like that?"

"I don't fuckin' know, but she got the right bitch today. She's selfish as fuck anyway and don't care about nothing but fucking dick. Po' baby probably got sick from getting ahold of something she shouldn't have because her sorry ass Mama don't pay her any attention. Shit, po' baby can't even piss on the pot or talk right because Charaty don't even interact with that damn child. Fuck that bitch, since she saying how she feeling. We were never friends. All she do is use me anyway."

I started texting that bitch a piece of my mind back and was cut off when I heard...

"To replay your voice message, press one. To delete and re-record, press two. To send your message, press pound."

I pressed pound and hung up with no regrets. That hoe spoke from the heart and I did too. I was tired of being nice to a bitch who loved dick over everything.

Chapter Twenty-Two

Karmyn

Since I had been attacked, I hadn't been back to my apartment. I had been staying at a hotel for the past couple weeks. Armis extended an invitation for me to spend a couple nights at his crib but I had refused. I hadn't reached out to O'Shara even though she had called and texted me a couple times over the past few days wanting to meet up for drinks at our favorite happy hour spot. I didn't think I could face her after being attacked by the man she told me she was in love with. I know that what happened to me was at no fault of hers, but I couldn't face her at the moment, or maybe ever again.

I wondered in the back of my mind if Enzo had ever been abusive to O'Shara. Neiysha had told me that he liked to dip in that good ole booga sugar, and I could see that he was under the influence of something the night he attacked me. I took a deep breath as I exited the freeway, making my way to my apartment complex. I felt that me going by there today would give me the closure I needed to move on in life. I felt that it would be best for me to move to another location. I had a feeling Enzo attacked me because I was friends with both of his bitches. I didn't know if he would resurface and try to attack me again, especially being that he was still involved with them both to my knowledge.

I pulled through the back gate in search of my assigned parking space, and that's when I noticed the swarm of police officers and the news crew. Hopping out of my ride, I walked over to a neighbor who lived not too far away from Neiysha and I to ask them what was going on.

"She's dead. Maintenance went in for a service order she placed for the dishwasher and they found her dead. The downstairs neighbor complained about water leaking from their ceiling," the older woman whelped.

"Wait, who's dead? What happened?" I tried to walk through a gap in between the buildings that led close to my apartment and was immediately cut off by law enforcement.

"That's where I live? Why is there crime scene tape around my apartment?" I screamed.

I could feel my stomach turning in knots. I watched the crime scene unit come from around the corner with a body bag on a stretcher. I fell down to my hands and knees and emptied the contents of my stomach in the wet grass. *Oh my God!* I screamed inside. If I would've told the truth about what happened to me that night, maybe I could've saved Neiysha's life.

My ringing cell pissed me off as it vibrated in my purse. I didn't and couldn't talk to anyone at a time like this. I noticed that it was a number I didn't have saved but did look familiar. I answered anyway, hoping it would miraculously be Neiysha.

"Hel— hello?"

"Hello, Ms. Thompson. This is detective Sanders; I was wondering if you could by chance meet me down at my office within an hour or so. I have some more questions for you regarding your attack. I came by your apartment, but you were not home."

"Is that— is that Neiysha that's dead? Tell me, please tell me that's not her!"

"Are you here, Ms. Thompson? I see you, I'll walk to you."

Detective Sanders darted my way and helped me from the ground.

"He did it, didn't he? That evil monster attacked me and killed her. I should've told you who attacked me, and I could've saved her life. Oh! I'm such a horrible person. I'm so sorry, friend!"

Chapter Twenty-Three

Between that dumb ass nigga blowing her up and Charaty fake ass calling and texting to apologize every day, O'Shara was about ready to smash my phone into pieces.

"What?!" Shara screamed, finally answering her phone after ignoring the continuous calls from the jail that day.

"Shar, baby, please just listen to me. I'm so sorry, this wasn't supposed to happen to us," Enzo cried his heart out, hoping that she could forgive him.

Shara rolled her eyes as her heart stung, not noticing that her new man had just got to their new crib and was walking up behind her.

"Us? Us! Ha! You should've thought about that before you did the dumb shit you did," she emphasized, trying hard to hold back tears.

"Just come see me please. Just this once, and I promise not to ever bother you again. I really need you right now."

"I don't know about that. I don't think that's a good idea. Look, I have to go!" Shara hung up the phone, feeling Rashaan's presence in their bedroom.

Rashaan walked up to his woman and wrapped her in his strong arms, inhaling her sweet scent.

"What's up, boo? I missed you while I was running in these streets today. What you up to?"

"N-nothing, baby. Just going over the paperwork for the new training class I'll be teaching next week. I'm kind of nervous though," O'Shara admitted.

"I'm sure it's going to be fine, boo. Don't stress, everything will work out in your favor," Rashaan comforted his woman by pulling her into his lap as he sat next to their king-sized bed in his lazy boy.

"You're right, boo. I've just been thinking too much into it." O'Shara relaxed, leaning back on her man's chest, playing with his ear lobe. "So, what you wanna eat tonight, babe?" O'Shara asked.

"Shit, besides you?" Rashaan laughed. "Hell, I'm not sure. Let's go out though. It's a new Asian spot downtown, my homeboy said it's what's up. Let's check it out."

"Ok, babe. Lemme go change real quick."

O'Shara went into the couple's walk-in closet and began to search through the hanging clothes for something more comfortable to change into.

Ring! Ring!

She rolled her eyes and exhaled as she placed her cell in her ear without checking the caller info.

"Yeah? Man, ok. I'm on the way to you but can't stay long. Rashaan and I are going to dinner."

"Everything good, babe?" O'Shara's new boo asked as he approached the closer doorway.

"Yeah, babe. Well, I don't know. That was Char. She asked if I could come by for a minute. I told her we were on our way to dinner and--"

Rashaan cut her off. "Babe, go ahead and see about your friend. It's cool, we can order in."

"But-" O'Shara started again.

"Go ahead, boo. Do you need me to ride with you?"

"No, it's ok, I won't be gone long." She stood on her tip toes to kiss her man's soft lips before grabbing her keys and leaving out the house.

Rashaan locked the door after his woman left in a hurry. He felt that by O'Shara going by Charaty's for a bit, it gave him enough time to set up his proposal. He had been running around all day picking up the perfect trinkets to make their night special; the best champagne, chocolate covered berries from Ms. Grad's kitchen, and the finest, prettiest rose petals.

About thirty minutes after his boo left, Rashaan lined the walkway from the front door to the master bathroom with candles and rose petals. He went back into the bedroom to search for his cell to text O'Shara and see how close she was before lighting the candles. As soon as he found his phone on the dresser, he could hear ringing from the couple's closet. Confused and not quite knowing what was going on, Rashaan walked to the closet and found the ringing came from his girl's cell. When he saw her best friend's name flash across the screen, he quickly answered thinking that O'Shara could be calling from Charaty's phone after realizing she left out the door without it.

"Aye, what's up?"

"Thugga? Hey, this is Charaty. I thought Shar would've been here by now." She laughed, not ready for his response.

"Yeah, I did too. I see she left her phone. Damn, I hope everything good with her. If she's not there within the next ten minutes, hit her phone back for me."

"Ok, sure I will."

When they disconnected the call, Rashaan snatched up his girls' phone and the keys to his truck. Swiftly, he made his way to the front door of their new home and outside to his whip. His first thought was to gun it towards Charaty's house to make sure his lil boo wasn't stranded somewhere on the side of the road.

He jigged in his ride, cranked the engine and threw his truck in reverse. As soon as he entered the highway towards Charaty's crib, O'Shara's line rang again, this time from an unlisted phone number. Without thinking, and hoping it wasn't his boo calling his for aide, Rashaan slid the green icon with his thumb and placed the phone on his ear.

"You have a collect call from an inmate at the county jail. To accept please press—"

Before the prompt finished, Rashaan pressed one to accept the call.

"Aye, boo. Can you come up here please? Shara?"

***

Not even twenty minutes later, O'Shara was pulling up to the county jail. She found a parking spot and got ready to kill the engine and hop out, but the radio stopped her in her tracks.

"Local detectives now say that Enzo Thomas, who was charged with the death of thirty-year-old Neiysha Johnson, charges will be increased. Authorities now say that after the autopsy of Ms. Johnson, details show that she was with child."

"With child. With child?" O'Shara let out a wail that was not human.

She jumped out her ride, being sure to grab her wallet and darted across the Rocky gravel to the big red building. Pulling the double doors open, she walked in slowly. Trying to keep her composure, she walked over to the shortest line to check in for visitation. After handing over her identification to the sheriff that sat behind the glass and putting her info in the system, she made her way down the hallway to the elevators.

O'Shara's stomach bubbled as she rode up to the 4th floor. Sweat beads dripped down her neck, and she suddenly felt queasy when the elevator dinged, alerting her of her arrival. When the doors pulled open, O'Shara's body tensed up smelling the remnants of inmate feces and only God knows what else as she walked to her assigned window number 3.

Up until this moment, she didn't even notice there were others on the elevator with her and also in the visitation room. Hearing the heavy, metal doors slam shut shot chills down O'Shara's spine and slapped her out of auto pilot mode.

She looked up and saw the line of offenders walking towards their designated seats behind the glass. When Enzo's face appeared in the window O'Shara almost lost her breath. As bad as she wanted to curse his bitch ass out, she couldn't. Her emotions overflowed and uncontrollable tears rushed down her face. Enzo's gut fluttered at first when he saw the only woman he's ever loved beautiful face. O'Shara gritted her teeth while gripping the hell out of the nasty ass black phone that hung to the right of the window.

"Shar, baby, please," Enzo begged, not quite knowing what to say at a time like this. He knew he had fucked up. Not only his relationship with O' Shara, but his life.

"First of all, I'm not your fucking baby. I ain't shit to you."

"Really? Really? That's how the fuck you feel? I did this for you, for us. If—"

"Oh, *if*? Ha!" O'Shara laughed sarcastically.

"If what? You killed your pregnant side bitch who was carrying your child."

"Ma'am!" An officer shouted to calm O'Shara down. She nodded her head in understanding and stared into her ex's eyes.

"Pregnant? Nah, that hoe wasn't pregnant by me." Enzo scratched the back of his head and lied through his teeth as if the woman he had been with all his life couldn't read right through him.

"Ok. Here we go with the lies. Look, I don't have time for this shit. I'll be changing my number today, so you will never be able to contact me again. I don't hate you at all because everything happens for a reason. My first thought was why. I felt like I needed to know why you would stoop as low as this to end someone's life. Was it because you were scared that your little secret would get out? Or are you just an evil bastard?"

"I'm not evil, but I was greedy. I guess I just couldn't take the fact that the one I loved found something better than me, something you really deserved. And the one I was cheating with had been fucking over on me, so I was fucked up about the whole situation and snapped."

"Look, I wish you the best through your double life sentence. Live your fucking life because I'm finally living mine!"

O'Shara slammed the phone back on the receiver and stood to walk away. As she made it down the hall to the elevators, she felt like a huge weight had lifted from her shoulders. She was ready to start her new life with her new man, a real man.

After retrieving her I.D. from the desk officer, O'Shara made her way across the street back to the parking lot. She almost shitted bricks when she looked up and saw Rashaan parked next to her ride smoking a blunt while he leaned on his truck.

"Hey, babe, I—" O'Shara started and was quickly cut off as she expected to be.

"I just came to bring you your phone, Charaty called." Rashaan laughed sarcastically and handed his soon to be ex woman her cell.

He turned away from O'Shara and started walking around the bed of his ride.

"Wait! Baby just hear me out real quick," Shara begged, wrapping her arms around Rashaan's waist.

"Hear what?" Rashaan's deep voice boomed. He turned around and pushed her hands away.

"You lied to my fucking face, dawg, ain't shit to talk about."

"Rashaan, Rashaan, fucking listen to me!"

"I'm gone man, fuck this shit, Shar! I ain't been nothing but good to yo' ass. But that's not what you want, huh? You want a grimy ass nigga who gon' steady treat you like shit, so go hold that nigga down. I'm done!"

Rashaan walked away again, finally making it to the driver's side of his truck. O'Shara blocked the handle of the door with her body, stopping Rashaan from leaving and pissing him off even more.

"You aren't going anywhere until you hear me out. Now I'm sorry for not being truthful about where I was going, but I've never lied to you about anything else. I love the fuck out of you, I don't want that sorry ass nigga."

"Yeah, what the fuck ever, man. Move! Go visit yo' nigga!"

"See, nah you fena piss me the fuck off. You wanna know why I came here today? To rub in that nigga face that I am happy with the man I'm with and even happier about the family we will have. You know how I know that you're the nigga for me? Because I'm carrying your fucking baby, Rashaan! After many years of being unable to conceive, I am pregnant, nigga ,with yo' lightbulb head ass baby. So, if you want to leave, fine, go, but you will take care of this damn child!" O'Shara screamed full of emotion.

"Pregnant. You're pregnant?" Rashaan smacked his lips. "Man, gone on. You fucked up and trying to clean this shit up."

"Ok, since you think I'm lying, ask him. Just ask that nigga what I told him?" O'Shara answered her cell as another incoming call from the county jail came through. She put the cell on speaker so Rashaan could hear Enzo crying out like the bitch made nigga he was born to be.

"Aye, my man said you need to stop calling me."

"Look, I just wanna wish y'all and the baby the best. Ain't no hard feelings. And tell him I apologize about his fam, man. I get it, and I won't call anymore."

"Now goodbye! And I'm changing my fucking number, so your bitch ass won't call anymore!" O'Shara shouted before ending the call.

"I'm sorry for being dishonest with you, Rashaan, but you will not come at me sideways. Now anything else, nigga?" She folded her arms and cocked her head towards her baby daddy.

Rashaan stood across from his woman speechless. He didn't know what else to say. The way O'Shara's feisty ass just checked him had his dick wanting to poke her thick ass right there in the parking lot.

"Man, bring yo' ass here!" Rashaan pulled O'Shara to his chest, covering her with his arms.

"I don't want anybody but yo' ass, nigga. You know that." She laughed, burying her face into Rashaan's chest. "Let's go, baby. I'm hungry."

"Ok, boo. Hop in the truck and I'll have my potna come pick up your ride. But first…." Rashaan took a step back and stared at his woman. "Shar baby, I love you. Like for real though. I got upset because besides my child and our family, I don't want to share you with anyone else, ever. You're my everything, babes. And to know now that you're carrying my seed, that just makes me feel better about making this decision. I was preparing for when you got back from your girl's house to do this, but I don't want to wait any longer. O'Shara Marie Arthur, will you be my wife? I want you to marry me girl!" He asked, dropping to one knee and opening the ring box.

O'Shara jumped out the passenger seat of the truck where she sat and ran into Rashaan's arms.

"Yes, baby! Fuck yeah, I would love to be your wife! Oh, my goodness!" O'Shara jumped off her man. Rashaan slid the blinged out rock on her left hand and swallowed O'Shara's lips with his.

***

As Enzo walked back to his cell, he could hear cheering from the fellow inmates on his block.

"Man, what the fuck you niggas so crunk for?" Enzo asked his cellie.

"That nigga just proposed to that fat booty bitch right there in the parking lot!"

"And she said yes!" Another inmate shouted out messily.

Enzo focused his eyes through the window where he saw O'Shara and Rashaan filled with glee and happiness. Seeing her completely open and affectionate with another nigga they both knew treated her better stung his heart, but he understood that it's what she needed and deserved.

EPILOGUE

"Now friend if you don't stop sweating this make up off I'ma charge you triple!" Karmyn joked with O'Shara as she blotted away more sweat beads on her forehead.

O'Shara the blushing bride stood in front of the vintage mirror nervously.

"I'm sorry boo. I told that nigga we should've waited until after the twins came to get married. I know I look like a damn whale up in this dress."

"Girl hush you look beautiful!" Charaty chimed in and she burst through the dressing room door with a chilled bottle of water for her best friend.

"Whatever Char you're just saying that because you love me."

"I'm saying that because it's true! And because I love you. Now hurry up everyone is waiting on you to show off all this fine!" Charaty tried pumping her best friend up again.

Being that O'Shara was almost six months pregnant with twins now she felt uncomfortable on her wedding day but would have to just suck it up and push through her feelings because she and Rashaan agreed to be Mr. and Mrs. before the birth of their children. After finally getting herself together, she was ready to walk down the aisle to become Mrs. Rashaan Leroy Johnson.

***

Charaty sat at the table scarfing down shots as she watched Armis freely dance with Karmyn wrapped in his arms.

I can't believe this gay ass nigga. Charaty spoke to herself watching them in disgust. At first, she acted like she was cool with the whole ordeal of her first love being a male booty bandit, but deep inside it bothered her.

When the DNA test came back and proved Samad was Ahmani's father, on top of Armis and Karmyn being an official couple, Charaty decided to put her feelings for him to the side and let him be.

As long as she didn't have to see them together, she was cool about it, but today had a bitch in her feelings.

Armis had the one he truly loved, and O'Shara was finally with a man who gave her the world, and all Charaty had was Ahmani, so she was being salty.

Charaty stood from the table she sat at to make her way to the bar again to get another round of shots when she was interrupted by the music stopping and the DJ calling her name over the mic.

"Charaty Glenn! Is there a Charaty Glenn in the building?"

She turned around with wide eyes and watched as the large crowd stared at her.

"Yo baby daddy said bring yo ass up here girl. He wanna rap witcha for a second."

The crowd laughed as a shocked and confused Charaty drug her heavy feet to the front of the reception hall.

Standing there was Samad dressed in a tailor-made suit waiting on his woman with a microphone in his hand smiling.

"Come on baby. We've waited long enough, it's time for us to make this shit official. I love you and only you and—"

"She love your ass too brother!" O'Shara shouted out as she rocked in her new husband's arms.

"I know she do sis. Baby I want you to be mine. I'm through with all the other bullshit." He dropped down to one knee and opened a small velvet box.

"Baby Mama—" he stopped in his tracks when Ahmani approached him.

Charaty stood back with tears in her eyes not knowing what to say. Even though she loved the way Armis made her feel sexually, she's always truly loved Samad.

"Mommy please marry my daddy!" Ahmani's adorable voice screamed over the mic.

Charaty walked over to both of them and pulled them into her arms.

"Yes baby. Mommy will marry yo daddy!"

Samad slid the blinged out rock on Charaty's left hand and pulled her into a kiss.

"I love you Samad. I always have and always will."

"I love you too baby. Always and forever."

THE END!!

Thanks for reading! Please leave a review via Amazon, or Goodreads!

Authoress Ms. Grad Marie's Catalog

Share my World with a Savage Like You 1&2 **Complete Series

Stealing the Heart of a Dirty South Hustla' 1-3 **Complete Series

Diary of a Single Mother, Standalone Novel

Love Heist: He robbed my heart, Novella

A Thin Line Between Baby Mama And B*tch!

Ash & Omar: Forever Loving A Dirty South Hustla', Standalone Novel

Hooked on a Fifth Ward Menace 1&2** Complete Series

She Fell in love with a Southside Dopeboy, 1&2

Caught up in the Wrath of a Hitta's Love (Episode One)

When a Gangsta Falls for a Real One, *Standalone novel

All titles FREE with Kindle Unlimited Subscription!!

https://amzn.to/2Br9g95